MW01137682

LOUIS AND ZÉLIE

LOUIS AND ZÉLIE

The Holy Parents of Saint Thérèse

WRITTEN AND
ILLUSTRATED BY

GinaMarie Tennant

IGNATIUS PRESS SAN FRANCISCO

Cover art and design by
Christopher J. Pelicano

ISBN 978-1-62164-371-5 (PB)
ISBN 978-1-64229-150-6 (eBook)
Library of Congress Control Number 2020946495
Printed in the United States of America ♾

To my parents,
Ed and Lisa Tennant,
my Louis and Zélie

CONTENTS

I

A SOLDIER'S SON

LOUIS, ARE YOU READY?" Madame Martin asked as she stepped into her son's room.

"I am having trouble with these buttons," the seven-year-old responded.

Madame Martin bent down to finish buttoning his coat. "Now you look like a soldier's son," she said as she straightened. "Remember your hat. I will be waiting for you at the front door."

Louis picked up his hat and placed it on his head carefully. Then he made himself as tall as he could and said, "Turn about, forward march!" Louis strutted out of his room.

"Louis, you look so funny!" his little sister giggled.

"Fanny, stop it! I am being Father."

"No, you aren't. You are too short. Your coat and hat are wrong, and you don't look like him."

"Someday I might."

"I thought yesterday you wanted to be a missionary."

"Maybe I will be both."

"Children!" called their mother.

Louis and Fanny ran down the stairs. "Louis, we must be leaving. We have errands first. Fanny, obey the maid, and don't bother Marie." Madame Martin leaned over to kiss her four-year-old daughter. "We will have a surprise for you and Marie when we return."

Louis and his mother walked out onto the busy street. "What will we get Fanny and Marie?"

"You shall see."

The streets of Strasbourg, France, were crowded in the year 1830. Madame Martin grasped her son's hand tightly as they threaded their way through street vendors, customers, and gossipers. Words in French and German filled the air. The timber-framed houses had overhanging upper stories that cast shadows in the narrow streets.

Madame Martin stopped in front of a store. The hanging sign showed a clock.

"Is this where we will get the girls their surprise?" Louis asked his mother.

"No, this is the shop of our friend Aimé Mathey. He will fix our clock."

As Madame Martin and Monsieur Mathey conversed, Louis wandered around the store. He longed to touch the gears and the pendulums lying on a table. *Assembling a clock must be like putting a puzzle together or like playing with building blocks*, he decided.

"Louis, would you like to see how a clock works?" asked Monsieur Mathey.

Louis looked up at Monsieur Mathey. "Yes, please."

Monsieur Mathey picked up a small clock with its back missing. "Push the pendulum," he said.

Louis did as he was told.

The shiny pendulum swung back and forth. Inside the clock it moved a gear, which moved another gear and then another one. As the different gears moved they caused the hour and minute hands to move on the face of the clock. Louis stared at it, fascinated.

Monsieur Mathey said, "If one little thing goes wrong, it will not work correctly."

Louis nodded his head slowly. "Thank you, monsieur. You must know a lot."

The sun was warm as Louis and Madame Martin stepped out of the dim shop. Madame Martin led the way toward the cathedral. The magnificent reddish structure had been built centuries before. It was dedicated to Our Lady, Notre-Dame.

The cathedral was cool inside. Madame Martin walked part of the way toward the altar. She knelt down and was soon absorbed in prayer. Louis knelt beside her and recited the Our Father and the Hail Mary, but he could not concentrate. All he could think about was clocks. *I guess people are like clocks—when we sin we do not work correctly. Then we need Jesus to fix us.*

Madame Martin leaned toward Louis. "Would you like to light a candle?"

"Yes, please."

Madame Martin handed Louis a coin. "Here is an offering."

There were several people lighting candles. Louis waited patiently. His eyes wandered around the cathedral. His family often visited it, but he still marveled at the gothic pillars, the stained-glass windows, the ceiling high above the altar, and the astronomical clock. He decided he would make a detour to see the clock after he lit his candle.

"Are you waiting to light a candle?" an elderly woman asked.

"Yes, please." Louis dropped his coin in the metal container. *Kerplunk!* He glanced around to see if anyone had been disturbed, but no one seemed to have noticed. He lit a candle.

For whom am I lighting this candle? he wondered. *Hmm . . . I will light it for my family.*

Louis walked halfway across the cathedral to the

clock. Even though the clock had been broken for decades, Louis found it fascinating. Not only had it told the time of day, but it had told what day of the year it was and where the sun and the moon were in the sky. At the base of the clock was a globe of the night sky. Panels of paintings decorated the area surrounding the clock's mechanism. Louis could figure out what some of the paintings portrayed: Creation, the resurrection of the dead, and the Last Judgment. Others he did not understand. There were statues on the clock that had once moved when the clock struck noon.

Louis sighed. *I wonder if Monsieur Mathey could fix it.*

Finally, Louis went to find his mother. She was not where he had left her. He looked at the various people praying. *Mother is wearing a blue coat*, he reminded himself. *There she is*, he decided. He crossed the cathedral again. The woman turned—she was not his mother! He saw another woman in a blue coat; he followed her only to be disappointed once more. A clock outside chimed noon. *If I don't find her soon, we will miss Father!*

Louis decided the best place to go was where his mother had last been. He sat down. "Dear God, please help her find me. I know I should not have wandered. I am sorry. I won't do it again." He wanted to cry, but he was not going to. He was the son of a soldier; he would behave like one.

"Louis, there you are." Madame Martin hurried toward him. "Where were you?" she whispered.

"I am sorry. I went to see the clock."

"I should have known."

The sound of drums and bugles could be heard as Madame Martin and Louis stepped out of the cathedral. People of all ages crowded the sides of the road. Madame Martin and Louis quickly found a spot where Louis could see the street. The music was getting louder.

"Mother, am I in trouble?"

Madame Martin was silent for a moment. "No. It was partly my fault. I should have trusted you to return. Unfortunately, actions have consequences. We did not have time to buy you the paints. On the way home we have time either to purchase the paints or to get the girls their surprise. What do you think we should do?"

Louis had been eagerly looking forward to having his own box of paints. To have to wait longer would be hard, but he could not disappoint his sisters. He had only one choice. "We can wait on buying my paints."

"That's my good son." Madame Martin patted him on the shoulder.

The parade of soldiers could be seen in the distance. Louis forgot his disappointment as he watched the soldiers come toward him. Then they were right in front of him. The band played a stirring march as the soldiers filed by in time to the beat. Louis saw his father, Captain Pierre-François Martin, pass in front of him. He was sure no boy ever had a father so brave and handsome as his. The captain had been on several campaigns and had traveled as far as Poland. The most recent was the Spanish campaign when France had intervened to restore the King of Spain to his throne. He had returned from it decorated with the Cross of the Knights of Saint Louis, a prestigious military honor. *Surely the army thinks Father is brave since he is the town's adjutant, helping them run this city by being in charge of correspondence*, Louis thought.

When the parade had disappeared from sight, Madame Martin led Louis out of the crowd and down a narrow street. Louis did his best to keep up with his mother's steps.

"Mother, aren't you proud of Father?"

"Of course. No woman has a better husband than I have. Your father is a good and faith-filled man. He works hard for God, France, and his family. Some of his soldiers once asked why he knelt at Mass for so long after the Consecration. Your father said, 'It is because I believe.' That is the way he lives his whole life."

Louis was silent for several minutes. "Mother, you are wonderful. I know Father thinks so too."

Madame Martin smiled. "He has always thought that. When I was a young woman, your father wanted to marry me; however, my father had lost his fortune. A woman needs money to get married. It is called a dowry. Since there was no money for the dowry necessary to marry an officer, your father paid the dowry."

Madame Martin opened the door of a French pastry shop.

"Is this where we will get Fanny and Marie's surprise?" asked Louis.

"Yes. Which pastries do you think the girls would like?"

Louis helped his mother pick out a cream-filled pastry for Marie and a chocolate-filled one for Fanny. His mouth watered as he looked at the sweets. Louis walked along the display case, trying to decide if any of them looked better than his favorite, a chocolate-filled pastry. None did.

Madame Martin finished her purchase. Louis followed her out of the store. They passed a crippled man in rags sitting in a doorway. Madame Martin stopped. She pressed a coin into his hand and handed him a chocolate-filled pastry. The man's eyes shone in disbelief.

"Madame, are you sure?"

"Yes. Please enjoy it."

"Thank you, thank you, and God bless you."

"Mother, you gave away Fanny's gift," Louis said as soon as they were out of the man's hearing.

"No, I didn't. That was mine, and the man will enjoy it much more than I would. Fanny's pastry is still in here, and so is yours."

"Mine?"

"Yes. You did not think I would neglect you, did you? It is your favorite: chocolate filled."

"Thank you, Mother!" Louis beamed. "When we get home, I would like to share mine with you."

"You do not have to share it with me."

"I would like to give you some."

"All right, I will accept a small piece. Thank you very much."

Fanny and ten-year-old Marie were delighted with their surprises. Louis and his mother had picked the perfect sweets. Louis gave half of his pastry to his mother. He ate his half slower than usual. Somehow this one tasted better than any he had eaten before.

That evening, when the family gathered in the drawing room, Captain Martin entertained the children with a tale of the orphans of Berezina. The Berezina River in Russia was the site of a disastrous battle for the French in 1812 during Napoleon's retreat from Moscow. The children of fallen French soldiers had to brave many odds to survive. Louis had heard the story before, but it thrilled him every time.

Madame Martin put away the socks she was darning. "Fanny, it is time to get ready for bed." She took her little girl by the hand and led her toward the stairs.

Captain Martin smiled at his wife, Fanie, and little Fanny. Then he started to read some papers of his own. Marie and Louis settled themselves at a table to draw. Too soon the clock in the hall struck eight.

"Time for bed, Louis," Captain Martin said.

Louis looked at Marie. She was allowed to stay up longer. He reluctantly put away his art supplies. "Good night, Marie. Good night, Father," he said as he slowly walked up the stairs.

Madame Martin was leaving the girls' room. "Good boy, Louis," she said. "Do you need help with the buttons?"

"Thank you, Mother, but I think I can undo them. Mother . . ." Louis lapsed into silence.

"What is it?"

"Mother, what do you want me to become?"

"What do you mean?"

"When I grow up, like Father. What do you want me to be?"

Madame Martin was silent. He was just a little boy. Would he understand what was really important in life: to know, love, and serve God by following His commandments and always responding to God's personal call? She smiled. "I want you to be a holy man."

"Like a saint?"

"That's it. Exactly."

2

ZÉLIE AND HER MOTHER

NINE-YEAR-OLD ZÉLIE GUÉRIN was sewing. She had pushed her chair as close as possible to the sitting room window for light. The setting sun shone on her brown hair. It was several days after Christmas in 1840, and the cold drafts by the window made her shiver. She pulled the shawl around her tighter.

"Ow!" Zélie had pricked herself. She looked at her

finger. It was not bleeding. So she continued sewing the dress she was mending.

Sounds of chatting and laughter came from outside. Zélie stopped working and looked out the window. A mother and her three daughters were walking along the street. The older two girls were laughing together, and the youngest girl was clutching her mother's hand. They seemed so happy. When the littlest one turned slightly, Zélie saw a doll in the girl's other hand. Zélie sighed—she so wanted a doll. It did not matter what size to Zélie: a tiny one would suit her fine.

"Zélie, have you finished the mending?" asked Élise, her sister. Élise had on a large apron that made her look small for her eleven years.

"Almost." Zélie's dark eyes sparkled with tears. "I wish I had a doll."

"It is no use to wish. You know Mother does not bother about dolls and toys. Finish your sewing quickly, then come join me in the kitchen. We will think about something cheery. I am peeling apples for supper. I bet you can guess what I am making!"

Élise left, and Zélie resumed her sewing. When the dress was mended, Zélie neatly put away her sewing supplies and carried the dress upstairs to the bedroom that she and her sister shared.

Zélie looked around the shadowy room. *It would be so much nicer if we had toys and dolls in here.* Suddenly she smiled; she knew what she would do! She took a shawl and carefully laid it on the bed. Then she folded a small towel into an oval and placed a handkerchief on one end of it. Finally she folded the shawl over the towel and had it encircle the handkerchief.

It looks a little bit like a baby doll dressed for the cold. It will be fun to show Élise. Oh no! I am supposed to be helping her. I hope I won't be in trouble. Zélie ran toward the stairs.

"Zélie! Walk. Do not run," her mother, Madame Guérin, yelled from the kitchen.

Zélie stopped and slowly walked down the stairs. She joined Élise and their mother in the kitchen.

"Zélie, you have been dawdling. Do you think God likes that? You had better say an Act of Contrition. I am going upstairs. Help Élise with the meal."

Zélie said her Act of Contrition and then put on an apron. She sliced bread, stirred the soup, and helped Élise with the apple tart. That was Élise's surprise.

The outside door opened, blowing a gust of cold air on the girls. Their father, a policeman, walked into the kitchen. Zélie helped him take off his snow-covered coat and boots. She hung the coat up to dry.

"Where is your mother?"

"She is upstairs."

Monsieur Guérin went to see her. Zélie, sniffing the delicious aroma of the apple tart baking, started to set the dining room table. She was looking forward to the meal.

Monsieur Guérin returned. "We are to have dinner without your mother. She needs to rest."

The meal, as always, started with a prayer. Élise, in

the absence of Madame Guérin, dished up the food. They ate in silence. The sisters noticed that their father seemed worried. Finally Monsieur Guérin broke the quiet. "This soup is delicious. It reminds me of my mother's cooking and my childhood."

Élise smiled. "Father, please tell us again about your uncle the priest."

"Yes, please," Zélie added.

"Some other time." Monsieur Guérin resumed eating until he saw Zélie's crestfallen face. "No, I will tell you now. It is always good to recall Father Guérin.

"As you girls know, I was born at the start of the French Revolution. The churches were closed, and the religious were being hunted and guillotined. Father Guérin was staying at my family's house. I was only a boy, but I was given the job of escorting him around the countryside to visit the Catholics.

"One day when we were both home, soldiers knocked on our door. My uncle hid himself in the kneading trough, a large basin my mother used to make bread dough. When my mother opened the door, the soldiers angrily pushed her aside and began searching the house from top to bottom. I knew the kneading trough was an obvious place for them to look. I got some toys, sat down on the trough's lid, and started to play. Those soldiers never got to look inside the trough."

"Father, you were very smart and brave," Zélie told him.

"Father Guérin was quite brave. One day he was carrying the Blessed Sacrament, and three scoundrels attacked him. He placed the Holy Eucharist on a nearby rock and said, 'Lord, take care of Yourself while I deal with these rascals.' He knocked those three men down and threw them into a shallow pond. Then he picked up the Blessed Sacrament and continued on his way. Those three scoundrels emerged from the pond soaked and defeated. It was the last time they disturbed my uncle.

"He was finally captured and imprisoned. After many years he was released, and he became a parish priest again."

"I am glad I did not live then," Zélie said.

That night Élise led the way to their room holding a candle. "Why are your clothes on the bed?" she asked Zélie.

"Can't you see what it is?"

"No. What is it?"

"It was supposed to look like a doll, but . . . I guess it doesn't," Zélie said with a sigh.

"Not really. Maybe someday Mother will give you one. Mention it to God tonight in your prayers."

Zélie put her clothes away in the chest. The girls got into their nightclothes and knelt to say their bedtime prayers. Zélie made hers extra long since she was requesting a doll. Then they climbed into bed. Soon they were fast asleep.

Zélie dreamed that she was in a large, lovely house. A beautiful woman stood in front of her, handing her a doll. Zélie was so excited. She had a doll! She happily cradled her gift.

"Wake up, Zélie!" Élise's voice floated into the dream. "Zélie, it's morning! Time to get up!" Élise seemed to be right above her.

"I have a doll," Zélie said with her eyes still shut. "A beautiful lady gave me a doll."

"You must be dreaming."

Zélie opened her eyes and looked at her arms. She was hugging a blanket, not a doll. She was in her bedroom in her own house, and there was no beautiful lady. It had all been a dream.

~

Several days later, on January 2, 1841, Élise and Zélie were sent to an elderly neighbor's house to bake for her. Élise rolled the dough while Zélie mixed the sweet topping. Oh, it smelled so good that it made their mouths water!

A knock sounded on the front door. Their neighbor hobbled out of the room to answer it. Zélie took the opportunity to ask the question that she had wanted to ask all morning. "Mother did not look well this morning. Do you think she is all right?"

"I think so."

"She is normally well, unlike me."

"We should pray. Let's say an Our Father and a Hail Mary for her."

It was late that evening when Monsieur Guérin came

to bring them home. Élise and Zélie rushed to the door to greet him.

"Is Mother all right?" they asked.

"Yes." He seemed quite happy. "Girls, you have a baby brother!"

"A baby brother?"

"Yes, a fine, strong boy."

"When can we see him?"

"Tomorrow. Your mother and the baby are sleeping."

The next morning, Zélie and Élise got up as soon as they saw the first signs of light in the east. The house was silent. They crept downstairs and prepared breakfast. Finally their father appeared.

"Can we see the baby now?"

"Yes, come along, but be very quiet—he's asleep."

Madame Guérin was awake and resting in bed. Beside her in a cradle was a little red face peeping out from layers of blankets. *He is darling,* Zélie thought, *and so tiny.*

"What will he be named?" Élise whispered.

"Isidore," Madame Guérin responded, "after your father."

I got my doll, Zélie thought happily.

To her disappointment, Zélie quickly discovered that baby Isidore was not to be her doll. Madame Guérin believed that Zélie was too young and inexperienced to handle him. Instead of helping take care of the baby, Zélie had to do more of the housework.

Isidore grew into a cute little boy. Unfortunately,

Madame Guérin spoiled him. It was hard for Zélie to watch her little brother get whatever he wanted and know that she had never been treated that way.

One day naughty Isidore was told to stay in the cellar until someone called him. It was a punishment for a mischievous deed he had done. Madame Guérin was in the kitchen while Élise and Zélie were sewing in the sitting room. Suddenly they heard Isidore shouting. "Mama, the cider is pouring all over the floor! I pulled the cork out of the barrel!"

Madame Guérin, Élise, and Zélie spent the next hour cleaning the cellar. Isidore was sent upstairs. When they had finally scrubbed the stone floor clean, they found Isidore quietly playing in the sitting room with some wooden blocks. It bothered Zélie that Isidore never got in trouble for having made the mess. *If I had done that at his age, Mother would have been so mad.*

Another day Madame Guérin, Zélie, and Isidore went to the market to shop. Zélie carried the basket while her mother made purchases. Isidore happily watched some geese in cages; no one paid much attention to him.

"Where is Isidore?" Madame Guérin said when she had finished her shopping.

"I don't know." Zélie looked around the crowded marketplace. "There he is, near the apple seller."

"Go get him."

"Isidore, it is time to leave." Zélie went to the boy and led him by the hand back to their mother. Several people smiled at the darling little boy. He smiled in return.

Madame Guérin shepherded her children out of the crowd. "What is in your pocket, Isidore?"

Isidore put his hand into his pocket and pulled out a juicy red apple.

"Where did you get that, Isidore?" Madame Guérin looked sternly at him.

"I got it from the apple stall."

"How?"

"I took it."

"You took it!" Madame Guérin grabbed his other hand and marched him back to the stall.

That time Isidore got in trouble, and Zélie did not feel sorry for him.

One day when Zélie was twelve, her father announced that he was retiring from being a policeman. "For thirty-five years I have been either a soldier or a policeman, and it is time I do something else. We will move to nearby Alençon. It is a much bigger town than this village of Gandelain. There will be good schools for you, children."

And so the Guérin family moved to Alençon. Monsieur Guérin bought a house on Saint Blaise Road. It was a rather small house, but he planned to enlarge it. Shortly after the move, Élise and Zélie were enrolled as day students at a nearby convent school.

It was the first time Zélie and Élise had been with so many girls their age. Both girls were shy. Fortunately, the religious sisters were kind and made the new students feel comfortable. Zélie soon discovered composition was her best subject. Out of her eleven papers, she won first place ten times in Advanced Composition. She also excelled in the lace-making class. The town was famous for a special type of lace, point d'Alençon. The convent was passing the profitable craft on to the next generation.

It was fascinating for Zélie to learn how simple thread could become beautiful lace. Lace making was different from the dull mending of clothes. Each piece of lace took a long time to make, but the finished product was intricate and lovely. It looked as if it were fit for a queen to wear. Her mother's sewing lessons had been worthwhile, Zélie decided.

What Zélie and Élise enjoyed most about the school was being with the religious sisters. The girls saw how the Faith was more than just rules: it was a relationship with God. Each day the girls went to Mass and spent time praying in the convent chapel. Zélie felt at home.

One day Zélie and Élise were walking through one of the school corridors. Zélie stopped in front of a beautiful statue of the Blessed Mother. "Élise, I've always wanted a kind and gentle mother." She motioned to the statue. "Jesus did give me one. She is His Mother —and mine!"

3

LOUIS' JOURNEYS

THE PATH WOUND ITSELF UPWARD as far as Louis could see. On one side of him the ground sloped downward sharply; on the other side it rose until it seemed to touch the sky. In the valley there had been fir trees and civilization; here there were only alpine flowers and rocks. Louis stopped to scan the magnificent Swiss scenery. In all his twenty years he had seen nothing like it.

I wonder if chamois live around here, Louis thought,

thinking of the goat-like animal that lives high in the Alps. After watching an eagle soar over his head, he gazed back to the path and saw, to his surprise, a strange creature on the path in front of him. The sun's brightness made it hard to see the creature clearly, but it looked small and heavy.

The creature was coming closer. *Is this animal dangerous? I'm alone, and all I have is a stick. What do I do? Perhaps I should leave the path and let the animal pass.* There were some large boulders a short distance above him. *I'll go up there.*

Louis started to climb toward the rocks. Pausing, he looked at the creature. It had stopped. Suddenly it turned around and began to run back the way it had come. The animal was running toward something lying on the path.

Louis climbed higher to see better. *I think that's a person! Maybe a monk!* Louis gasped. *Is the animal going to attack? Has it already? Oh no, what can I do?*

Louis quickly started to retrace his steps to the path. In his hurry, he missed a rock and stumbled. He managed to catch himself with his walking stick. He looked at the creature. The animal was standing over the man!

Suddenly the man sat up and patted the animal on its head. *It's a Saint Bernard dog!*

The man saw Louis and waved. Louis waved in return, feeling very relieved, breathless, and somewhat embarrassed. The dog left his master and started running toward Louis, barking a greeting. The monk followed the dog. Louis walked toward them.

Up close, the dog appeared gentle, friendly, and quite harmless. He wagged his large tail enthusiastically while Louis patted him on the head. Together they made their way toward the monk.

"Welcome, traveler. I am Father Augustine." The priest held out his hand. "I hope we did not surprise you."

"Just a little bit. I am Louis Martin, of Alençon, Normandy, France. It is a pleasure to meet you."

"It is my pleasure. Are you planning to spend the night at our hospice of the Great Saint Bernard Pass on your way to Italy?" the Augustinian monk asked.

"Yes, but I am not traveling to Italy; my destination is your monastery."

"Barry and I will accompany you there. I was training him to obey my commands. A lot of training goes into enabling these dogs to save so many lives. So you're from Normandy, in France; I was there years ago," the priest said, reminiscing. "Has it changed much?"

"Not much in my time. I lived there from age seven and a half. I was born in Bordeaux; then my family lived in Avignon and Strasbourg. We moved to Alençon when my father retired from the military. For the past year I have lived in Rennes, Brittany, to study watchmaking."

"I have never been to Brittany, but I have always wanted to visit. What is it like?"

"I really like Brittany, and I shall miss it, but it is time for me to have a different instructor. In Rennes I lived with some cousins. The region's culture is fascinating. I bought one of their traditional outfits and enjoyed wearing it. It consisted of a black coat, a light-colored vest, and very full pleated pants. If the weather is stormy the farmers wear wooden clogs. Brittany has its own language, which is related to Welsh."

"Isn't the government trying to suppress their language?"

"Yes, which makes the people use it all the more. The Bretons are very religious. Their literature contains miracle plays, and ballads. Reading their folktales is very enjoyable—their characters are so heroic."

Louis was very interested in hearing about the famed monastery at the Great Saint Bernard Pass. They kept climbing higher and higher. As the path led them up into a pass between two mountains, the valley was lost from sight.

"The road we are on was traveled by the ancients," Father Augustine told Louis. "See those stones up there? That was part of the Roman road. After the fall of the Roman Empire, this place became a hideout for robbers. Around 1050 a deacon named Bernard lived on the other side of the pass in Aosta, Italy. He became very concerned about the plight of the travelers, so he started this monastery and hospice to help them. More recently, the monks here began breeding and training dogs to help them rescue people lost in the snow. Our most famous dog was Barry."

"Surely you don't mean this dog!"

"I certainly don't. We name the most prospective

pup of each litter Barry in honor of our first Barry. That Barry saved the lives of forty people."

"Brittany has their heroic folktales, but Switzerland has their heroic dogs," Louis mused as he patted Barry.

"There is the hospice," Father Augustine announced.

Louis looked ahead to see a stone building several stories high. Beyond it a crystal-clear lake sparkled in the sunlight. The air was fresh and clear. Louis felt as if he were at the top of the world.

Louis was cordially welcomed by the other monks, who offered him food and a place to sleep. He joined the monks for the Divine Office and Mass in the morning. After Mass one of the monks showed Louis the ruins of a nearby Roman temple.

"The monastery and its grounds are so peaceful and quiet. It makes me feel close to God," Louis said.

"I am glad. Did you hear the dogs barking this morning?"

"Yes."

"So it isn't always quiet here. And we have avalanches —they are very loud. Some of the monks remember when Napoleon crossed this pass. It was very noisy then. To feel close to God, what matters is not where you are but who you are."

Louis felt sad when it was time to leave this beautiful and holy place. As he was preparing for departure, he stood outside admiring the terrain. He was struck by the beauty of the tiny alpine flowers. They looked so small and fragile, and yet how hardy they were. Louis reached down to pick a small white flower. He would put it in a book to press it. He would always have it.

~

It was time for Louis to resume his studies. He traveled to Strasbourg, where he was warmly welcomed by the Mathey family. Monsieur Mathey had consented to be Louis' next watchmaking instructor. He was also teaching his son and namesake, Aimé, and another student from Brittany, François.

On the first evening at supper, Monsieur Mathey asked Louis why he had chosen this profession.

"Your shop and the cathedral clock fascinated me as a little boy. I have always liked doing intricate things with my hands. I also enjoy drawing and painting. I thought watchmaking would be a good profession for me."

"Watchmaking requires an enormous amount of patience."

"I hope I have that."

"From what your parents wrote, I think you have what is needed to become a successful watchmaker. For inspiration, tomorrow morning you and Aimé should go see the cathedral's clock."

~

Early the next morning Louis and Aimé started out for the cathedral. It was enjoyable seeing the town after so many years. Louis noticed, as he had as a child, that the inhabitants of Strasbourg spoke both French and German. "I will have to relearn German," he told his companion.

"It won't be hard," Aimé replied. "I have lots of friends who speak German. You will be speaking it before you realize. François can already say simple sentences, and he has not been here long."

"That gives me hope."

"You will like Strasbourg. Wait until you meet my friends. We have a lot of fun times together. There is Lange, who has such long legs that he runs up the stairs four at a time. When we race he always wins, but he can never tell a joke from a fact."

They turned a corner. Louis stopped walking and looked at the magnificent building in front of them. "There is the cathedral."

"Yes. Does it look the way you remember it?"

"Yes and no. It is smaller than I recall."

"Or maybe it is just that you are bigger." Aimé grinned. "Wait until you see the clock!"

Louis reverently genuflected after entering the sacred building. It was good to be in church. He followed Aimé toward the clock.

"What do you think?" asked Aimé.

Louis stood still, awestruck. Finally he spoke. "What happened to it? It's different. It works!"

"Yes. They just finished this new one in late June. It took five years. Father knows the man who led the construction. For fifty years the man had wanted to work on the project, and he finally got his wish!"

"He must have been delighted." Louis silently looked at the new clock and all of its features. No longer could he dream of fixing the old one. Oh well, he had another dream. He thought of the peaceful monastery on the Great Saint Bernard Pass.

"See that?" Aimé interrupted Louis' thoughts as he motioned to a display of the sun and the moon. "That shows where the sun and the moon are right now and when there will be an eclipse."

"That is amazing."

"We will return here someday at noon to see the statues of Jesus and the apostles march around the front of the clock. A life-sized cock crows thrice during it."

"Incredible. I look forward to seeing it."

"I'll ask my father to introduce you to the man who led the construction. He can tell you all about the workings of the clock. If only I had been more experienced I could have gotten a job helping to build it. Maybe someday we will be the ones repairing it. Do you want me to show you some of the other important sights in town?"

"Well . . . no, not right now. I thought I might attend Mass. I think one is starting soon. Your father said we could take our time this morning. I have so much to thank God for: a safe trip, the chance to study, a place to stay with friends. Isn't prayer the best way to end or start anything?"

"I don't know . . . I have never had much interest in religion. It is rather boring, and it seems that we can be good without it." Aimé looked uncomfortable. "Today isn't even Sunday. But you go ahead. I'm hungry; I'll get something to eat and meet you here afterward."

Louis knelt down in the church, stunned. It was hard to grasp how someone raised in a good Catholic family, like Aimé, could have no interest in religion. For Louis, life made no sense without God. After Mass, Louis lit two candles, one for his family and the other for Aimé.

Monsieur Mathey was a good teacher. Louis learned to assemble clocks and watches, and he worked in the shop. Monsieur Mathey would tell him, "A successful watchmaker knows how to take care of clocks and his customers."

He taught Louis how a wound-up spring released its energy via the gears. The pendulum regulated the speed of the energy being released to keep accurate time. If the pendulum was not the correct length, it would make the clock go too fast or too slow. There were many intricate parts of a clock that had to be just so; when all was correct it needed to be wound only occasionally to keep accurate time. Each clock case was decorated as a piece of art, sometimes with wood carvings or ornate metal sculptures, and other times with painted scenes. Every clock was a mechanical and an artistic work. The more Louis learned, the more he realized he needed to learn. Many times he felt his hands were clumsy for the precise work, but he kept persevering.

~

On holidays Louis, Aimé, François, and some other young men would go for hikes in the countryside. They would pack a meal or purchase some food from a farmer's wife. These outings were eagerly looked forward to by all the friends.

During a hike on a hot summer day, they stopped for a swim. Louis was an excellent swimmer, and with easy strokes he was soon in the middle of the river. He then floated lazily on his back. The clouds formed interesting shapes. Birds flew across the sky. By turning sideways he could see the tree-lined bank and his companions splashing each other. Louis swam back toward them.

Aimé, splashing wildly, met him partway. "Can I stand here?"

"I think so." Louis placed his feet on the riverbed. "Yes."

Aimé, panting, uprighted himself. "How are you such a good swimmer?"

"My older brother drowned when he was little. My parents made sure I became a good swimmer."

"I'm sorry." Aimé was quiet as he caught his breath. "You've never talked about him. What was your brother's name?"

"Pierre. He was named after my father. Pierre was four years older than I."

"That's so sad. It is important to know how to swim well. Would you teach me?"

"Certainly. Let's go to calmer water."

The sun was high in the sky before Louis and his friends decided to get out of the water.

"Where is Aimé?" François asked.

"He is out there in the middle of the river," Lange responded. "He is trying out the new things you showed him, Louis."

Louis looked toward Aimé nervously. Aimé was not a strong swimmer yet, and he was sometimes rash in making decisions.

The other young men started to climb onto the bank, but Louis headed toward Aimé. Suddenly Louis tensed: Aimé seemed to be floundering! He was frantically splashing—and then he disappeared!

"Aimé is drowning!" Louis yelled to his friends on land. Louis started swimming faster than he had ever swum before. He tore through the water at lightning speed, keeping his eyes on the spot where Aimé's head had vanished. Where was his friend? He skimmed the nearby water with his eyes and let out a sigh of relief. There was Aimé! He was a short distance in front of him—Aimé's arms were struggling to get him afloat.

A moment later, Louis was beside Aimé. He grabbed him, trying to pull him up for air. Aimé, panicking, clutched Louis so tightly that they both went under.

Desperately Louis tried to free himself. He needed a breath of air. How could he save his friend if he himself drowned?

"Help, Lord!" Louis gasped for air as he came up. He struggled to raise Aimé's head but was dragged down again. "God, I can't do this alone!"

Louis tried to pull his friend toward what he hoped was land, all the while fighting to get a gulp of air. "God, help!" Louis' feet hit the bottom of the river.

He struggled to get himself erect—his head came above the water! He could stand! Aimé's grasp had weakened. Louis pulled him above the water. He heard splashing coming toward them. The river current was trying to knock them both into its depths again. He knew he did not have the strength to fight the current much longer, much less make it to shore.

The splashing was getting closer.

"We're coming!" someone shouted.

Then his other friends were surrounding them. Hands took Aimé from Louis, and other hands guided Louis toward the bank.

Louis was pulled onto the shore. He lay on the ground, panting. "Please, God, let Aimé be all right."

Lange leaned over Louis. "Aimé is breathing. He will recover."

Louis nodded weakly. "Thank you . . . all of you . . . and God."

François found a farmer who was willing to drive

them back to Strasbourg on his hay cart. Louis and Aimé were helped onto the soft hay; soon they were in Strasbourg.

Monsieur and Madame Mathey could not thank Louis enough for saving their son's life.

Louis smiled. "God gave us the strength. I was afraid at times that we wouldn't survive. God is due the praise."

~

Louis spent two years in Strasbourg with the Matheys. The day came when Monsieur Mathey told Louis that he had taught him all that he could. It was time for Louis to finish his apprenticeship elsewhere. Louis left Strasbourg, but instead of going home to Alençon, he went back to the Great Saint Bernard Pass in Switzerland.

During his time in Strasbourg, Louis had thought and prayed about his future. He had kept thinking about the monastery at the Great Saint Bernard Pass. *What a blessing it must be to live a life dedicated to God and service to your fellow men.* Louis had always felt a strong attraction to the priesthood, and to become a priest and live a monk's life attracted him even more. He was going to ask for admittance at the monastery. He had written to his parents and told them his plans. As always, they had said how much they loved and missed him and that they would feel blessed to have their son in God's service. They were praying for him. Louis knew he was blessed with wonderful parents.

He was warmly welcomed at the monastery by the monks and the dogs. The prior received him kindly and asked him many questions.

"Do you know Latin?"

"No, Father. I know only French and German. But I am happy to learn Latin."

"To join this monastery you need to know Latin already, since we don't teach it here."

Louis left the monastery. He would study Latin with a priest in Alençon. Surely the monastery would accept him in a few years when he would be fluent.

His parents eagerly welcomed him. It was so good to see them again. They both looked older. His mother had gray hair peeking out from under her cap, but her joy-filled face was still youthful. And although his father had more wrinkles, he still looked as distinguished as always: his white hair and sideburns only added to his appearance. Louis had not realized how much he had missed his parents.

Louis made arrangements for lessons in Latin with a local priest and bought a textbook. He spent hour after hour studying and memorizing words and grammar rules. Learning Latin was very different from learning German.

"Louis, you need to take a break from studying. Go for a walk or something," Madame Martin suggested, looking worriedly at her son.

"Mother, I have this chapter almost finished."

"You have been saying that for weeks. You need some fresh air; otherwise you will get sick."

"I will take a walk this evening."

~

Louis lay in bed, sick. Madame Martin came into his room with a cup of hot chocolate. She placed it on a table.

"How are you feeling?"

"I feel better than I did yesterday."

"Good. Drink this." She handed him the cup. "Later today you should be well enough to sit up some. But no studying."

"Mother?"

"Yes, Louis?"

"Maybe God is not calling me to be a priest. I can't seem to grasp Latin. Maybe this illness is the sign I am looking for."

"Father and I would be honored to have you as a priest, but that is not what we care about most. What is most important in life is to do God's will with love."

Louis prayed fervently. Reluctantly, he realized that God did not want him as a priest. Upon his recovery and with a heavy heart, he sold his Latin books and made plans to resume his apprenticeship in watchmaking in Paris, where his maternal grandmother lived. She had been inviting him to visit for some time. Her response to his letter was enthusiastic. There was certainly room for him. Her son-in-law, Louis-Henry de Lacauve, Louis' uncle, echoed her thoughts.

Louis was warmly welcomed by his grandmother, his uncle, and his uncle's son, Henry, a cadet. Louis and Henry became great friends. It was good getting to know his relatives.

Paris in 1847 was turbulent. Louis could not help but contrast Strasbourg with Paris. The people in Strasbourg were busy working hard and growing their commerce, but many of them still held their faith dear. In Paris the elite disdained religion, and the poor found it useless. The motto was "Get rich." Many of the wealthy had no interest in helping their needy neighbors, and the poor were desperate. Secret societies controlled people and made them do things they never would have done on their own.

Louis' new teacher had a large workshop with many students. After the two-year break, Louis needed to refresh his memory and retrain his fingers for the intricate work. He applied himself studiously to learning.

One evening, as usual, Louis placed the pieces of the clock he was working on carefully in a drawer. After cleaning the area with the broom and dustpan, he put on his hat and coat and stepped outside.

It had been raining, and a cool breeze greeted Louis. It was delightful to have a breath of fresh air in Paris.

"Monsieur Martin, please wait a minute."

Louis stopped and turned. He saw one of his fellow students emerge from the shadows of a building.

"Good evening," Louis greeted him.

"Good evening. Since I was leaving only shortly before you, I thought this was an ideal time for us to become better acquainted. I always want to make newcomers welcome."

"Thank you very much." *That's strange; he is the least friendly person in the workshop.*

An elderly woman was standing at the street corner, selling apples. Louis bought an apple and handed her a coin. She started to look for a coin to give Louis his change.

"Keep it," he said.

"Thank you, thank you," she said, delighted.

Louis' companion picked up an apple and handed the woman the same kind of coin that Louis had given her. "Uh . . . keep the change," he muttered.

The two students crossed the busy intersection. The street was thronged with wagons, horses, and people. They turned onto a side street.

"Are you spending the evening at home?"

"Yes. However, first I am stopping at Our Lady of Victories. It is my favorite church in town."

"The paintings inside of it are beautiful, and the gold on them makes the church exquisite," the other man commented.

"I like how it honors the Blessed Mother and God's

triumph together. My father told me how the church was turned into a gambling house and a stock exchange during the revolution of 1789. The Cathedral of Notre-Dame was made into a temple dedicated to reason and decked out as a theater before being neglected and nearly demolished. What sacrileges! I am looking forward to the cathedral's restoration. What a blessing that God is merciful to us. Sadly, we don't always accept His mercy. France is in trouble."

"It certainly is. That is why I stayed to talk with you today. Some friends and I have a club devoted to charitable works. I thought you might like to join us. We have a meeting tonight, but you can wait until the next one to join us."

"It is nice of you to think of me; however, I shall have to think about it. I will see you tomorrow."

Louis walked quickly to the church and once inside knelt to pray. Something seemed funny about that student and his invitation. He had never been friendly before, and he certainly was not pleasant toward some of the other students. Maybe another student could tell him more about this man and his club.

The next morning, Louis arrived early at the workshop. He glanced around the quiet room. Only the teacher and Jacques, a fellow student, were already there. Jacques was the perfect person to ask! He had been there a while and he knew everyone.

"Jacques, good morning!" Louis strode over to Jacques.

Jacques smiled. "It is a fine day to be out of the rain."

"I have a question for you."

"Fire away!" Jacques grinned.

"What do you know about . . . I don't know his name! He is one of the students who works in the corner over there," Louis said. "He has dark hair, is of medium height, and often wears a gray coat."

"Your description would fit most of us! What else do you know about him?"

"He doesn't wear glasses or have a mustache."

"If I rattled off names, would you be able to recognize his?"

"I don't think so. It is very odd—he never told me his name."

"That's impolite! It sounds like François. He generally associates only with the elite. What do you want to know about him?"

"Just about him. He talked with me yesterday."

"Aren't you lucky. He has never acknowledged me. Shh . . . here come his buddies, André and Jean. They think they are too good to be with the rest of humanity."

Shortly thereafter the teacher rang a bell. The workday had begun. Today Louis was fixing springs, but he kept thinking about François, André, and Jean. They did appear to be conceited and rude, but Louis reminded himself that they might be nice men who were ignorant of the way their mannerisms appeared to others. *I will be on guard and let their actions reveal their true selves.*

Louis decided to leave quickly that evening, before

the other students. He was a block away from the workshop when he heard his name being called. He turned.

"Yes?" he said.

François and Jean were standing there. François spoke. "I wanted you to meet Jean, as we never have time to converse during the day. Don't you think the teacher works us too hard?"

"No. He is teaching us to be master watchmakers. The work is precise and difficult."

"Have dinner with us tonight: a friend is hosting an informal gathering. Come."

"Thank you, but my grandmother is expecting me home."

"Come, be a sport! Have a life! Don't hang around old folks," Jean said.

"No thank you. Have a good evening." Louis turned and continued his walk home.

After a couple of blocks, he suddenly remembered that his grandmother wanted him to buy her a new watering can. He would have to go back. Louis started to retrace his steps. He was relieved to see that François and Jean were gone.

Louis stopped in his tracks. He was sure he had just heard his name. He looked around but saw no one he knew. He could hear low voices talking nearby. *They must be in the alley right in front of me. What do I do? I think it is François and his friends! Is it safe to walk by them? How badly does Grandmother need her watering can?* Louis hesitated, thinking.

"Be patient," the familiar voice of François said. "I can convince anyone, but now we had better take this conversation elsewhere. Remember, our monetary issues will be solved after I nab him."

"I don't like this," another voice said. "He is too open and kind. Besides, he seems rather smart. He might ask questions. Will our secrets be safe?"

"André, stop your worries. He is the perfect kind: naïve and innocent, a country kid with lots of money," François replied. "But we shouldn't be talking here: people might hear us."

Louis stood for a moment, stunned. *They have a secret society and want to take advantage of me!* He left quickly so they would not see him. His grandmother would understand about the missing watering can.

"What happened?" his grandmother asked, after seeing his face.

"Some supposedly nice men invited me to join their charitable group. Thankfully, I was suspicious of them. They were lying! They have a secret society and want me since I am generous. There is so much evil here! Oh, and I didn't get your watering can!"

"Don't worry about my watering can; it can wait. Remember, where evil is, love can be all the stronger. Why don't you take a walk to Our Lady of Victories Church and pray for those men. It will help you and them."

"I will do that, Grandmother," Louis said, and left for the church.

The church was quiet and peaceful. He knelt down. "Lord, thank You for showing me their evil intentions. What do I do now?"

Louis felt the answer quietly inside of him. "Confront the evil. Tell them that you are not interested in secretive things. Remember, you are on God's side. Do what you can, and let God do the rest."

The next morning Louis broke the news to the men. "I don't approve of secret societies; they control people. That is why it is wrong to be in them. It is too bad your club is not what you said it was."

François feigned surprise. "Whatever gave you the idea it is a secret society? All we do is help the poor—"

"No," interrupted Louis sadly, "don't try to fool me. And don't ask me to join."

Louis was very relieved that the men never mentioned it again. Now all he could do was pray for them.

Paris grew more turbulent as the months progressed. In February 1848, a fight broke out in the streets. King Louis-Philippe abdicated the throne to create peace and passed the crown to his nine-year-old grandson. However, the people were far from pleased; they proclaimed a republic. The leaders bickered while the people continued to suffer. In late June civil war erupted in Paris. The archbishop, trying to stop the fighting, was killed. For three days the fighting raged.

Louis found that God was his one source of strength. He spent hours praying before the Blessed Sacrament. From Jesus he felt the courage to face numerous temptations. Every day he prayed that he might do God's will.

~

After three years of study in Paris, Louis became a master watchmaker. He would now be able to open his own shop. Louis returned to Alençon overjoyed. It was such a blessing to breathe the fresh air and hear the birds sing. His parents welcomed him joyfully.

A kind, prayerful woman, Mademoiselle Félicité Baudouin, helped him set up a shop in town. His store opened onto the street, and Louis and his parents moved into the rooms above and behind the shop.

As Louis hung his sign in the window, his father smiled and said, "You finally decided Alençon is to be your home."

"I didn't decide. God did."

4

TRIALS AND LACE

ÉLISE, ARE YOU SURE?" Zélie asked her sister.

"Of course. We cannot both leave home at once, and I am not ready to go yet. Mother relies on me so much with the housework that it only makes sense you go first."

"Thank you very much." Zélie put her hat on her neat bun. Then she left her bedroom and walked down the stairs.

Élise followed her sister. She thought of how her

dear, quiet, fun, but serious little sister had matured—she would make a great Daughter of Charity.

Zélie and her mother silently walked down the streets of Alençon; they were both deep in thought. As they stood in front of the convent, Madame Guérin surveyed her daughter, who now was of medium height and slender. *She's actually rather pretty*, she thought in surprise. "Zélie, your father and I are very pleased with you. We are proud to be giving our daughter to the Lord. We will be praying for you."

Zélie smiled. It was rare to hear praise from Madame Guérin. "Thank you, Mother, and thank Father." Daughter and mother clasped hands, then Zélie leaned over and gave her mother a kiss on the cheek. "I will try to live up to your hopes for me."

"I certainly hope you do. I have done my duty, trying to raise you to be a God-fearing woman—the rest is up to you."

As they walked into the building, a Daughter of Charity welcomed them. "Are you Marie-Azélie Guérin?"

"Yes, I am."

"Reverend Mother is ready to meet you."

Zélie took leave of her mother and followed the sister. She was so excited and yet so nervous. This was the day she had dreamed of for the last several years. Would the Daughters of Charity accept her? She longed to follow the footsteps of saints by praying and caring for the sick and poor. She thought of Saint Vincent de Paul and Saint Louise de Marillac, who had together founded this order, and of the Daughter of Charity to whom the Blessed Mother had appeared twenty years ago, in 1830, and given the Miraculous Medal. Zélie could almost feel the white winged cornette of the Daughters of Charity on her head.

"Welcome, Marie-Azélie," mother superior greeted her. "Please sit down. I understand you are called Zélie."

"Yes, Reverend Mother," Zélie quietly responded.

"Please tell me about yourself and why you think God is calling you to be a Daughter of Charity."

"I am eighteen. I was born in Gandelain on December 23, 1831. I was baptized in the parish church of Saint Denis-sur-Sarthon. I have a sister and a brother. My family moved to this town when I was twelve. My family is very religious. My parents taught me from the very beginning to detest sin. When I was twelve I started to go to the convent school of the Sisters of the Religious of the Sacred Hearts of Jesus and Mary of Perpetual Adoration. There I saw the peace and joy of being a religious. My faith really deepened at school, and I longed to serve God. I have considered many different religious orders and have decided that yours is the one for me."

"Why is that?"

"I would like to help people with my hands, not just my prayers."

"Being a Daughter of Charity is very hard work."

"I know."

"A sister is on her feet for hours caring for the sick. She is awake early and up late. She is around many diseases. She needs to be strong both spiritually and physically."

"Yes, I understand."

"Have you ever had ill health?"

"Yes, when I was younger. I was often sick and suffered from headaches."

"Have you had any gentlemen friends?"

"No, but I have an eight-year-old brother."

"You are a beautiful girl—gentlemen must have admired you."

"I don't think so. I hope not."

"That is no way to talk. Marriage is a beautiful institution, created by God, and it is a sacrament. There are many paths to holiness. What is important is that you follow the one God has chosen for you."

"Yes, Reverend Mother, of course."

"Come, let us go into the chapel and pray that God's will may be done."

Zélie, her heart pounding, followed the mother superior into the chapel. Was God not calling her to the religious life?

Upon leaving the chapel, the mother superior smiled at Zélie. "We shall both do a novena. Come back in nine days. I will tell you the answer then."

The next nine days seemed like eternity to Zélie. She prayed the novena and doubled her other prayers. She made many little sacrifices to God. At home she was extra kind and helpful to her family. On the ninth day, Zélie and Madame Guérin returned to the convent.

The mother superior smiled as Zélie entered. "Has God given you an answer to the novena, my dear?"

"I prayed only that God's will be done."

"Your faith means the utmost to you, I am certain. God calls some people to be religious, others to live virginal lives in the world, and others to marriage. Each call is beautiful. Zélie, God is not calling you to the religious life."

Zélie was speechless. God was not calling her to the religious life? How could that be?

The mother superior seemed to read Zélie's thoughts. "By embracing God's will, you are living for Him. I think there is a young man somewhere in this world who is perfect for you. Live a holy marriage: that will glorify God greatly."

Zélie and her mother left the convent sad. How could Zélie get married? She had no money for the necessary dowry because her family was saving their money for Isidore's education. Since moving to Alençon, money had not come easily. Her father was an amateur wood carver and was not paid well. Her mother had opened a café in the front of the house, but that had failed—not due to lack of good food but because of the lectures Madame Guérin had offered her customers.

Upon the women's return home, the rest of the family was also disappointed, but they reassured Zélie that she would figure out what God wanted of her in life.

"And in the meantime, you can help around the house," Madame Guérin told Zélie. "Whether you're cleaning floors in a convent or in this house, it doesn't really matter."

"I guess not."

~

On December 8, the Feast of the Immaculate Conception, Zélie stayed in the church praying after Mass. She went to the statue of the Blessed Mother and knelt in front of it. The statue had a beautiful smile, and its eyes seemed to be focused on Zélie. Zélie smiled in return. Her heavenly Mother must be willing to help her. She knelt in silence.

Then she heard an internal voice say, "See to the making of Alençon lace."

See to the making of Alençon lace? Of course . . . that was the solution! Zélie had been good at lace making in school, and there were professional schools in town at which she could perfect her skill. She could certainly make a living from lace making.

Zélie looked back at the statue. The Lady seemed to be smiling at her in a special way. "Thank you, Mother." She looked toward the tabernacle. "Lord, thank You. You do have a plan for me!"

At dinner that day Zélie told her family about her revelation. "I think I could earn a living by making lace."

"That is an excellent idea. You are a good seamstress," Madame Guérin told her.

"And a patient, meticulous worker," Monsieur Guérin added. "You will be a success."

Élise smiled at Zélie. It was obvious she thought the plan wonderful. Isidore kept eating his food.

Zélie enrolled at one of the professional lace-making schools in Alençon. There was much more for her to learn. At home she continued to perfect her work.

"You are still working on it?" Isidore questioned his older sister one day.

"Yes. There are nine types of stitches. Every lace maker specializes in one of them. Right now I have to learn them all."

"I can barely see your needles."

"Aren't they tiny? I am using them to weave and make knots."

"Interesting."

Zélie looked outside. It was raining. Her parents and Élise were at the market, and she and Isidore were home alone. What a pleasure it was to have him around on his holiday. Maybe she could use her lace making to create a guessing game for him.

"What do you think this resembles?" Zélie asked, showing Isidore the lace.

"I don't know."

"It is something outside."

"A flower?"

"No."

"A bird?"

"You're getting closer."

"A moth?"

"Almost."

"A butterfly?"

"That's it! Every piece of lace is made by lots of people. One person starts with a piece of parchment. A design is pricked onto it, a series of many dots. The parchment is attached to a piece of linen to make it more stable. See?"

"Yes. Then what happens?"

"The outline of the lace is made by using the holes, and then the design is created over the outline."

"The lace is such a small piece."

"One lace maker must join several pieces of lace together. That person also has to detach the lace from the parchment. It is very difficult and time-consuming. That is why only the wealthy can afford it."

Zélie looked at her piece of work. It looked finer than what she had made as a girl in school. Now it looked like fine strands of cobweb. *Maybe someday one of my pieces will be fit for a queen.*

"When is dinner?"

Zélie smiled. "You've had enough of lace making," she said, looking at the clock. "We'll start making dinner now. Come along."

~

Zélie returned late in the evening from class. Monsieur Guérin met her as he normally did at the school and accompanied her home. She was grateful for his presence, but this night she hurried upstairs to talk with Élise as soon as she arrived at the house.

"What is the trouble?" Élise asked as Zélie entered.

"Do you remember how I told you about the monsieur who runs the school?"

"Of course."

"I do not like the way he has been acting toward me. I feel he is always trying to get my attention. His praises and courtesies are obnoxious. I keep ignoring him. Today he made the whole class wait while he insisted I hear how his favorite rose plant died."

"What did you do?"

"I told him I was not interested in his personal life. I got up and found a new seat in the back of the room. What do I do now? I can't go back. Things will only get worse."

"Why do you have to return?"

"I can't find work on my own; I was getting it through the school."

"Why not start your own business?"

"Start my own business?"

"Yes. You know how to prepare the piece of parchment, make the lace's outline, and finish it at the end. You are good at fixing mistakes and rips in the lace. You could easily find nine lace makers to work for you."

Zélie hesitated. "I am shy."

"You are perfectly comfortable chatting with the peasant women we meet. You can do it. Let's discuss this tomorrow with our parents."

"Élise, I would need a market for the lace. I have no connections."

"There must be a solution to that. Let's say our night prayers together and ask for God's guidance."

Zélie found it hard to sleep that night. When morning came she nervously approached the breakfast table. She liked Élise's idea, but she felt it was impractical. Besides the marketing issue, no one in her family had run a successful business.

Monsieur and Madame Guérin listened quietly as Zélie, with Élise's help, told them about the director of the school and their idea.

"My main concern about running my own lacemaking business is getting customers. We don't know any of the wealthy people in town. They are the ones who would order lace. The simplest solution is to find a company in Paris that would commission the lace, but I am too timid to succeed in dealing with them."

"That is a predicament," Madame Guérin said.

"It really isn't, Mother." Élise spoke quietly but firmly. "I can go to Paris and find Zélie a company."

"You?" Zélie and her parents exclaimed.

"You are also shy," Madame Guérin reminded Élise.

"I know, but I am willing to do it for Zélie."

"I will accompany Élise to Paris," Monsieur Guérin told his family. "We will find you a company, Zélie."

The Guérins set up the front room of their ground

floor to be Zélie's office. The room that had housed their disastrous café was going to be hers.

Zélie made samples of her work to be taken to Paris. Élise and Madame Guérin prepared a wardrobe suitable for Élise to wear as a businesswoman in Paris. Just that year the train had come to Alençon. Traveling would be quicker than ever before; however, no one knew how long the business in Paris would take.

The day came when Élise and Monsieur Guérin left for the capital. Zélie stood with her mother and Isidore watching them depart. "Please keep them safe, God," she prayed.

"Someday I will go to Paris," announced her little brother.

"Yes, you shall, to study," Madame Guérin said. "You will be a success in life."

I certainly hope I am also a success, Zélie thought. Then her mind reverted back to Élise and Monsieur Guérin. *How long will it take them? Will Élise find a company? When will we hear from them?*

Élise's first letter home told them that she and Monsieur Guérin had arrived safely. Every day the Guérins in Alençon hoped for news of Élise's undertaking. Finally, several letters later, she wrote that a lace company called Maison Pigache would give orders to Zélie.

Madame Guérin smiled broadly and said, "Élise did it."

"We knew she would," Isidore exclaimed.

Zélie sat down in her chair, smiling. God had a plan for her life, and He was taking care of her. "Thank You, thank You, God," she prayed.

But the joy at the Guérin house did not last. Another letter followed shortly thereafter, written by Monsieur Guérin: Élise had gotten a severe chill, and he did not know when they would return.

In Alençon, the Guérins prayed earnestly for Élise.

When Élise and Monsieur Guérin finally arrived home, Élise looked pale but happy. "It's happened!" she told Zélie. "You have your livelihood!"

Zélie hugged her sister. "You have had to suffer so much for me. How can I ever thank you?"

"Pray for me."

Élise was right: she needed prayers, for she fell ill again. This time it was much more serious, and the doctor was called to the house. He emerged from Élise's room with a very grim face. The verdict was that Élise had consumption. She had three months to live.

Zélie was grief stricken when she heard the news. She was too miserable to cry. What did it matter that she had her business if Élise was dying? Why had she ever let Élise go in place of her? Élise had so wanted to become a nun, but she had kept putting her desire aside to help her family. "Please, God, spare her. Heal her so that she can become a nun."

Élise told her family that she was going to start a novena to Our Lady of La Salette for the purpose of asking that she might be healed enough to become a nun. Zélie joined in the novena.

One morning Zélie carried a tray of food to her sister's room. Élise was sitting by the window looking out at the beautiful day.

"How are you feeling today?" Zélie asked.

"Every day I feel better."

"You know what happened three months ago today?"

"I certainly do. The doctor came and said I had three months to live. It looks like he didn't account for prayer."

"Or God's will." Zélie set the food beside her sister. "When you are well, you will finally have the opportunity to become a nun."

"I hope God will find me worthy enough."

"Of course God will."

"I am no saint."

"That is why God is giving you a second chance, to become one."

Élise smiled. "He is calling you to be a saint also."

"But He doesn't seem to be calling me to be a religious sister."

"Probably not, but He has a plan for you."

"God keeps reminding me of that," Zélie said, grinning. "You had better eat your food before it grows cold. Mother is calling me. I will be back shortly."

Zélie left the room. She was so happy she felt like

singing. Élise was recovering! Someday Élise would fulfill her dream of being a nun. And as for herself, Zélie had the whole world ahead of her.

5

THE BRIDGE OF SAINT LEONARD

LOUIS STOOD in the crowded Parisian railroad station, waiting in line for the ticket seller. His business had been completed sooner than he had expected, and he had a day to spare. It was rare for him to make sudden plans, but he had already sent his parents a telegram.

"Monsieur, where to?" the man at the ticket window asked him.

"One ticket to Strasbourg."

It would be good to see his friends and the city again. What a surprise it would be for Aimé and his family. He would spend one night in Strasbourg and still make it to Alençon on the day he had planned. Louis boarded the train.

After Louis disembarked from the train in Strasbourg, he found his way easily to the cathedral. Then Louis bought some gifts and walked to the Mathey watchmaker shop.

It looked practically the same. Various watches and clocks filled the display window. He glanced within: Aimé was helping a customer. He would not see Louis enter. Louis opened the door and stepped inside. He faced the window and looked intently at a watch winder on display. Aimé would come shortly to see who the new customer was.

"How may I help you, sir?"

Louis turned toward the voice.

"Louis!" Aimé gasped, delighted.

"Aimé! It is great to see you."

"What a surprise!" Aimé embraced Louis. "Whatever brought you here? Why didn't you tell us that you were coming? We would have had an entourage meet you at the station. How long can you stay?"

Louis smiled. His friend still loved to talk. "I can stay only for the night. Then I must be traveling back to my shop."

"Then we will have to celebrate your visit quickly. Wait until you meet my wife and daughter!"

Aimé took Louis upstairs to visit his parents and to meet his wife and baby girl. Supper that evening was very enjoyable. They laughed over old memories and talked about their businesses.

Aimé said, "My father must have almost given up on my becoming a watchmaker. I was so impatient."

"It just took time," Monsieur Mathey replied.

"For a while it seemed I also would not be a watchmaker, but it happened," Louis reflected.

"It certainly did!" Aimé exclaimed. "Tell us about that little piece of property you just bought."

"I call it the Pavilion. It is a garden with a hexagonal tower, three stories tall. The tower is my place to relax, read, and keep my fishing supplies."

"Do you still collect verses and place them on the walls?" Aimé wondered.

"Yes, but they are all religious ones now."

"You sound almost like a hermit!" young Madame Mathey said.

"Not quite, although it sounds appealing. I attend social gatherings, and I enjoy playing billiards. I am involved in several Catholic associations, including the Vital Romet Club. It is named after Vital Romet, a friend of mine. We have deep discussions and do charitable works." What a shame, Louis thought, observing his friend's reaction, that Aimé still seemed to have no interest in religion. *He is missing so much.*

"You are not married?" Madame Mathey asked. "Surely you are planning to get married. You must be in your thirties."

"I am thirty-four, but I have no intention of marriage. God has a place for bachelors also." Louis smiled. "My life seems rather full."

The visit in Strasbourg came to an end all too soon. The Matheys fondly bid good-bye to Louis and wished him safe travels. Aimé's baby, playing with a rattle Louis had given her, waved. The family gave Louis letters and presents for his parents, and Aimé told Louis to give his greetings to François, their old friend.

"I will. I played the same trick on him at his shop in Brittany as I did on you."

Then all the clocks in the shop began chiming nine o'clock. Louis knew he needed to hurry to the train station. "Good-bye! Thank you!"

~

Zélie sat in her family's little garden. It was an unseasonably warm March day in 1858. She had decided to piece the lace together outside. She had placed a chair and a small table in one corner of the garden. From her position she could see all that happened in the back of the house.

It is a shame that I am so unhappy, twenty-six-year-old Zélie thought. "Ouch!" She looked down at her freshly pricked finger. She felt that it served her right for being so selfish. For years she had supported and encouraged Élise in her dream of becoming a religious, but now that Élise was almost ready to join, Zélie was miserable. Life without Élise would be almost unbearable. What should she do? Zélie stopped her work. "Dear God and Mother Mary, please help me."

Zélie finally gathered up her work and walked into the house to find Élise. Being with her would be a comfort.

Élise was sorting through articles of clothing in her room.

"Élise?"

"Zélie, what brought you in on this beautiful day?"

"I wanted to be with you."

"Dear sister, what are you going to do when I am no longer here?" Élise sounded very concerned.

"I will have to leave also," Zélie replied. She knew not where she was going to go or what she was going to do, but God must have another plan for her soon. He would take care of her. *My heavenly Mother will make sure I am cared for*, she told herself.

~

Louis had closed his shop early that day to go fishing. Accompanied by his dog, a greyhound, he walked to the Pavilion, collected his fishing tackle, and walked to a nearby stream. He found a pleasant spot to sit and cast his line. The greyhound wandered off to inspect some rabbit holes. Louis looked at the dainty clouds in the sky, the glistening water, a bird chirping nearby, a spider weaving its web next to him, and the small flowers surrounding him on the banks. *God's creation is awesome*, he thought.

Once he had a sufficient catch, Louis collected his dog and walked to the nearby Poor Clare Monastery. The nun at the gate profusely thanked him for the fish.

"You are always so generous, Monsieur Martin. God will bless you for it."

Louis returned to the Pavilion and put away the fishing tackle. He walked outside to his statue of the Blessed Virgin. The over-three-feet-tall statue had been a gift from his friend Mademoiselle Baudouin. The Blessed Virgin's arms were outstretched as if in blessing. He said a prayer. "Please help me to do your Son's will. Thank You, God, for all Your bountiful gifts." Then he and his dog walked back to the house. *I am certainly blessed*, Louis thought contentedly to himself.

~

Captain and Madame Martin had partaken of an early supper. Then Madame Martin left her husband reading and hurried onto the street. She was taking a class to learn her new hobby, point d'Alençon, and wanted to make a visit to church before class.

She sighed as she walked. Louis might be content with his life, but she was not content with it. At his baptism, an archbishop walking by had prophesied, "Rejoice; this is a child of destiny." Surely he was, but not much showed for it. Her four other children, Pierre, Marie, Fanny, and little Sophie, had all been called from this world. Marie and Fanny had both been married, and Fanny had had a little boy, who was now fourteen. At least there was one grandchild. If only Louis would find a woman he liked and get married.

She entered the cool, peaceful church of Saint Pierre de Montsort. She knelt to pray. "Almighty God, please help Louis find the perfect woman for him." She thought of one wealthy young woman they knew, Pauline Romet; her brother and Louis were good friends. Pauline had made it obvious that she liked Louis; he, however, had shown no interest in her. Madame Martin could understand why Louis did not desire to marry Mademoiselle Romet. She was a strong Catholic, but too worldly for him. Only a very special woman would suit Louis. There was a young woman in her lace-making class who was reserved, smart, and practical. Madame Martin had seen her at weekday Mass. She resolved to learn more about this young lady tonight.

~

Zélie had decided to take a class in lace making at another lace maker's house. Zélie was inspired by other workers' techniques. Most of the students in the class were older women who were learning lace making for a hobby. Zélie arrived early and found a seat in the back of the room. While waiting she worked on a piece of lace. Several other women, all much older than Zélie, were also there. They sat in the front rows talking. Once, Zélie thought she heard her name spoken by one of them. She arose, but then she decided that she must have been mistaken. Relieved, she resumed her work.

Alençon was going to host a lace exhibition in June. Zélie's Parisian company wanted her to submit the highest-quality work she could do. It was good to have this on her mind, since Élise was leaving in a few weeks.

After the class, she put her lace and supplies in her bag. She arose and courteously waited for an elderly woman to leave. Then she walked toward the door.

"Mademoiselle Guérin," called a familiar voice.

Zélie turned.

"I want you to meet a friend of mine, Madame Pierre Martin," the instructor said. "She is just starting lace making. I was telling her how you have your own business."

"It is a pleasure to meet you, Madame Martin."

"It is my pleasure," Madame Martin replied.

At that moment several women came over to speak to the older women, so Zélie politely bid good-bye and withdrew. It was a relief to have been able to excuse herself so easily, since she was uncomfortable talking to strangers.

~

Madame Martin returned home smiling.

"Fanie, what happened?" her husband asked.

"I learned a lot, and I made some acquaintances," she responded.

Louis was in the room, so she could not say more. He was reading *The Imitation of Christ.* She looked toward Louis. "How was the Vital Romet Club meeting this evening?"

"It was fine. We prayed the rosary and then we had a discussion on Saint Luke's Gospel."

She had dropped many hints to Louis about marriage. He had taken no notice. Even if Mademoiselle Guérin was the perfect lady for him, Madame Martin knew only God could set the stage for their meeting.

~

It was an ordinary April day; Zélie, returning home from visiting one of her lace makers, started to cross the Bridge of Saint Leonard. Her mind was occupied with thoughts of Élise becoming a Visitation Sister in another city, Le Mans, and lace. She had a lot of lace to make this week.

As she started to cross the bridge, she noticed a man walking toward her. There was something different about him: he looked dignified and reserved. He was tall with chestnut-colored hair and a beard, and his blue eyes were kind, gentle, and peaceful. For a moment their eyes met, then they both looked onward.

Suddenly, Zélie heard an internal voice say, "This is he whom I have prepared for you."

Zélie was stunned. She tried to look at ease as she continued across the bridge; however, her heart was racing. Her hands, clutching lace, were clammy, and she shivered despite the pleasant day. *Is he the man for me? What if I never see him again? Who is he?*

~

Louis turned around to watch Zélie walk into the distance. *There is something different and likeable about that young lady. Who is she? She did not seem to notice me at all. I wonder if I will ever see her again?*

Louis resumed his walk once Zélie was out of sight. He could not stop thinking of the young lady he had just seen. He wished he knew her.

~

Madame Martin listened eagerly as her son told her about the young lady crossing the bridge.

"She has a very pretty and thoughtful face. She is medium height, slender, with brown eyes and brunette hair. Her clothing was simple but beautiful. There was something different about her; she seems unlike any other young woman I have ever seen."

Madame Martin smiled. "She sounds very nice." She could not help but notice that the description fit Zélie Guérin well. She decided to arrange an introduction for them. A gathering of lace makers would be a natural opportunity for Louis and Zélie to meet.

~

Madame Martin arranged a small get-together for some lace makers at her house. She knew Zélie would find such an invitation natural and feel obligated to attend. Never before had Madame Martin been so excited and nervous over a party.

The day came and Zélie appeared at the party. Madame Martin, noticing Zélie was shy and uncomfortable in a crowd, engaged her in conversation. As they talked she slowly led Zélie toward Louis, who was standing near the doorway watching them.

"Mademoiselle Guérin," Madame Martin said, "I would like to introduce you to my son, Louis."

Zélie's heart fluttered as she saw who the man was in front of her. The man on the bridge! She smiled, and Louis Martin smiled back at her. It was hard to believe this was happening.

Louis was fascinated by Zélie. She seemed so much more appealing than any other woman he had met. She had the gentle and refined manner of royalty but without any hint of pride, and she was apparently very successful in her lace-making business and quite intelligent. Most of all, she had a peaceful demeanor. Zélie Guérin reminded Louis of the Blessed Mother.

Zélie was occupied the rest of the party talking with Louis. They had found in each other someone who shared a similar enthusiasm for God and His Church. Zélie was the last to leave the party. Louis told her as she left, "I will see you soon."

At home Zélie kept thinking of Louis. He shared her values and aspirations. She was looking forward to seeing him again.

Madame Martin made sure they had plenty of opportunities to become better acquainted. Louis showed Zélie his shop and the Pavilion. Zélie in turn invited Louis to meet her parents and Isidore. They attended Mass together in Zélie's parish of Notre-Dame.

~

One evening Louis was invited to the Guérin house for dinner. He decided it was the perfect time to ask his all-important question. Madame Guérin greeted him at the door.

"Welcome," Madame Guérin said. "Zélie is in the kitchen. She will be here momentarily."

"I am really looking forward to seeing Zélie, but first I would like to have the opportunity to talk with you and Monsieur Guérin," Louis told her.

"He will be here shortly," she responded.

Madame Guérin led Louis into the sitting room. He felt he was being scrutinized by Zélie's mother and was glad when Monsieur Guérin appeared. Monsieur Guérin greeted Louis in his normal gruff but frank manner. They sat down, and then there was silence. Zélie's parents looked at Louis expectantly. The time had come for Louis to speak, and he felt at a loss for words. Finally he gathered his thoughts and spoke abruptly. "I have come here to ask for your daughter's hand in marriage."

Monsieur Guérin smiled. "I know Zélie thinks very highly of you, Louis, and likes you a lot. I am confident you will be a good husband."

"Yes, definitely," Madame Guérin added. "I hope you will get along better with her than I have."

"Then I have your blessing to propose to her?" Louis asked, holding his breath.

"Yes," Monsieur and Madame Guérin both responded.

Louis breathed a sigh of relief. Monsieur and Madame Guérin had consented! Now he had to ask Zélie if she would marry him. Suddenly he felt more nervous than before. Marriage had not been what Zélie had foreseen in life. Would she say yes?

"Now about her dowry," Madame Guérin said, "she is in charge of that. I know she is quite successful in her business."

It pained Louis to be jarred back to reality being reminded of the dowry that caused so many women anxiety. "I want Zélie regardless of her dowry."

~

Zélie observed that Louis was unusually quiet during the meal. Afterward Louis suggested Zélie show him the garden. She led the way to the small yard, puzzled.

Once again Louis felt tongue-tied. Zélie was telling him about the spring flowers, and he was barely listening. Finally he suggested they sit down on the bench in the garden. Zélie did so, looking worried. Louis was not himself.

The moment had come, and Louis found he had a voice. "Zélie, will you marry me?" he asked, hesitantly.

Zélie was quiet. Louis was asking her to marry him! He was gazing at her tenderly. Zélie smiled happily. "Yes, Louis, I certainly will!"

Louis' face broke into a smile bigger than Zélie had ever seen. He held out his hand to Zélie, and she gladly accepted it.

~

A few days later, Louis sat at a table in his shop sketching a picture. Various rejected drawings lay beside him. Was this one better? Yes, he decided.

"Louis, a letter arrived for you," Madame Martin said as she came into his shop.

"Thank you, Mother," Louis said, receiving the letter. "How does this look?" He showed her his latest sketch.

"It is beautiful. Is it for Zélie?"

"Yes. It is for the medallion I will hand her before I give her the wedding ring. I decided to depict a scene from the book of Tobit on it. The story of Tobias—his not being able to find a suitable bride, and Sarah's longing for a husband—describes Zélie and me well. They put their faith in God, and He fulfilled their prayers."

"He has answered our prayers."

"Yours," Louis joked. "I hadn't thought to ask."

After Madame Martin departed, Louis opened the letter. It was from Zélie. She was writing to tell him the day and time of the awards of the Alençon lace exhibition. Louis and his parents were looking forward to it.

~

June 20, 1858, was the day of the awards. The Martins arrived early and found a place to sit with Zélie's parents and Isidore.

The ceremony was lengthy, with elaborate speeches. Finally, it was time for the jury to announce the awards.

Zélie, trembling and nervous, was sitting with some of the other lace manufacturers. *It does not really matter if I win anything, but people would be so pleased if I did, and then my lace would be worth more.*

"A gold medal is awarded to Monsieur Jules-Pierre Beaumé, whose lace is innovative with three-dimensional effects. We like how he generously acknowledged his best lace makers. A gold medal is also awarded to Mademoiselle Marie Lépine for her fine, beautiful lace made in the traditional styles."

Zélie quietly sighed: her name was not listed among the gold medalists. Of course, she should not be disappointed; she had had her company for only five years. It would have been nice to win, but she knew that those companies deserved their awards.

The man kept speaking. "A silver medal is awarded to the Paris house of Pigache and Mallet, made under the direction of Mademoiselle Zélie Guérin."

I received second place! Zélie was overjoyed. All her hard work had been rewarded. The Parisian company would be pleased, so she would continue to get work, and her family and Louis would be delighted. She could hardly wait to write Élise and tell her the good news!

~

It was the evening of July 12, 1858. Zélie stood in her bedroom, surveying the familiar room. Her clothes and homemaking supplies were in trunks on the ground floor. Even her lace-making supplies were in parcels near the front door. She looked at the room a moment longer before departing for the stairs.

"Are you ready?" Monsieur Guérin asked, standing at the door with his wife and Isidore. They were dressed in their best clothing.

"You look lovely," Madame Guérin said.

Zélie smiled. Her dress, a lush dark color, matched her eyes. She had placed a collar of handmade lace around her neck and on her head a hat to match her dress.

The Guérins stepped outside into the shadowy evening.

Zélie clutched her purse. She felt thrilled and nervous at the same time. In just a few hours it was going to happen. She was going to marry Louis! *My good Louis*, she thought. *I am going to be Zélie Martin or Madame Louis Martin*. Both of those names seemed rather elegant.

They walked to the town hall. French law did not honor a religious wedding; a couple had to get married in the eyes of the government first, then they could have the religious ceremony. As was the current custom, Louis and Zélie would have their religious marriage at midnight, so they had scheduled the civil ceremony for two hours earlier, at ten o'clock. Louis and his parents were standing there waiting when the Guérins appeared. Louis smiled happily at Zélie.

Two hours later, at midnight, the large parish church

of Notre-Dame was lit with candles. Family and close friends of the Martins and the Guérins were assembled near the side altar.

Louis stood at the altar waiting. Out of the corner of his eye he could see Father Hurel also waiting. Then Monsieur Guérin escorted Zélie to the altar.

Louis looked at Zélie, his bride. There she stood: strong and beautiful. Zélie looked at Louis. His blue eyes were so gentle, earnest, and peaceful. Together they would live for God.

Before Louis put Zélie's wedding ring on her finger, he laid a medallion in Zélie's other hand. She looked at it. In front of a waist-high stone wall adorned with pottery and trailing ivy, Sarah and Tobias were walking toward each other and eagerly catching hands. Sarah had long hair and a flowing dress. Tobias had a staff in the crook of his arm and a hat hanging on his back. The couple was gazing into each other's eyes while Tobias' faithful dog was looking up at his master. Louis and Zélie's names were beneath the picture. On the other side of the medallion, Louis and Zélie's initials and their wedding date were surrounded by a delicately engraved floral wreath. Zélie returned her gaze toward Louis and smiled. She knew that the medallion said what Louis felt unable to express: how much he loved her and how God would guide them, like Tobias and Sarah, on their journey together.

6

ZÉLIE'S DOLLS

LOUIS AND ZÉLIE WALKED hand in hand one beautiful evening along the streets of Alençon toward the Church of Saint Pierre. It was late autumn; a cool breeze sent leaves swirling around them.

"How do you feel today?" Louis asked Zélie.

"Happy and excited! I guess that is not a doctor's type of answer!"

"I prefer your type of answer."

Zélie became thoughtful. "I have been thinking about names."

"So have I. I would like our child to be named after the Blessed Mother. If our baby is a boy, he could also have Saint Joseph as his patron, and we could call him Joseph: Marie-Joseph."

"What about Marie-Joseph-Louis? But if the baby is a girl what shall we name her?"

"How about Yvonne?"

"Yvonne? That is not a common name."

"It is, in Brittany."

"How about Louise? Marie-Louise. Besides being a feminine for Louis, both my mother and Élise had that name." Zélie paused, thinking of Élise's new name. Élise was now Sister Marie-Dosithée, which meant *Marie giving herself to God*. "I still sometimes forget to call Élise by her religious name."

"That's understandable. She only earned the Visitation habit early this year. I like the name Louise," Louis said, thinking of Zélie's mother. She had died two months ago, on September 9, 1859. It was obvious Zélie missed her mother, even though they had not gotten along well together.

~

Thursday mornings were Zélie's busiest time all week: the lace makers, whom Zélie employed, came to the house to exchange pieces of lace. The women had just departed when the fire alarm in town sounded. Fifteen-year-old Adolphe, Louis' nephew, rushed into the room from Louis' shop.

"There's a fire! Uncle Louis went to help!"

"Of course," Zélie responded nervously.

She said a prayer for Louis and those affected by the fire, and then she followed Adolphe into the shop. Madame Martin was there already. She was looking out the window.

"Is the fire coming this way?" Zélie asked.

"No, or at least I cannot see any smoke. Let's hope it's a small fire."

"Grandmother, may I go see the fire?" Adolphe asked.

"Yes, but do not be a hindrance to anyone, and be careful!"

"Yes, Grandmother." Adolphe hurried onto the street.

The two women were left in the quiet shop. Outside, men shouting, with buckets, ran one way while women ushered their curious children in the other direction. Zélie and Madame Martin were silent. Captain Martin came downstairs to join them.

"Another fire. We must trust God to keep Louis and everyone else safe," Captain Martin said solemnly.

Nobody said what they were all thinking. Louis was a member of the Alençon Volunteer Fire Department. Once, Louis had entered a burning building to save an unconscious woman. He had carried her through flames and out of the building to her frantic husband and children. What would happen this time?

It seemed ages until Zélie saw men returning. Some of them had soot-covered clothing. Anxiously she looked for Louis. Where was he? She still did not see him.

There he was! He and Adolphe were walking toward the house. Zélie opened the door and hurried toward them. Louis, her Louis, was safe! God had protected him.

~

February 22, 1860, was a very important day for the Martins. Marie-Louise was born.

Zélie lay in bed holding the little baby. *What a responsibility and a privilege to be a mother.* She looked in awe at the little girl and mused, *I finally have my own doll!*

Later that day Madame Martin and Louis took little Marie to the Church of Saint Pierre. Madame Martin carried Marie since Louis was too nervous. *He will get his practice*, Madame Martin thought contentedly. Captain Martin and Adolphe followed them. Zélie was at home, resting.

Father Lebouc, Monsieur Guérin, and Isidore greeted them at the entrance. They all walked to the baptismal font. Madame Martin and Monsieur Guérin were to be the godparents.

Louis looked at his little girl. Once he had so hoped to become a monk, and Zélie had dreamed of being a religious sister; instead, they had both been called to marriage. *What an honor it is to raise a child!*

He heard the priest say the holy words. "I baptize you in the name of the Father, and of the Son, and of the Holy Spirit." *Marie-Louise is a child of God!* "God, please help Zélie and me to be good parents."

Upon their arrival home, Madame Martin handed Marie to Louis. "Marie is asleep. You will get comfortable holding her. Remember, you used to carry little Sophie."

Louis carried Marie, layered in blankets, to Zélie.

She smiled eagerly at their entrance. "You're home! How is Marie?"

"Fine. She is sound asleep," Louis reported, handing the baby to Zélie.

Zélie cradled her little bundle. "Louis, I was thinking that instead of our child calling us by the formal names of Father and Mother, let us teach her to call us Papa and Mama."

"Well . . . that is definitely different from the way we were raised."

"I know, but I don't want Marie to have the troubles I had with my parents. I want her to have the childhood I wanted and to be comfortable with her parents."

"I agree. Let's use Mama and Papa."

~

Little Marie grew quickly. Zélie and Louis delightedly watched her learn to smile, crawl, and say "Mama" and "Papa."

Zélie liked to carry her to the large statue of the Blessed Mother that Louis had previously had in the Pavilion garden. At Zélie's request he had put the statue in a prominent place at home. Zélie would decorate the wall around the Madonna with blue fabric and lace for special feasts, and she would place vases of flowers next to the statue. "See, Marie," Zélie would say to her little girl, "look at Our Lady's hands: they are outstretched. She wants to help you. God loves you so much that He gave His mama to help you to be a good girl. Always remember that God loves you more than your mama and papa possibly can, and we love you so much."

~

On December 8, the Feast of the Immaculate Conception, Zélie woke up early. Today was a very important day: nine years ago the Blessed Mother had told her to make Alençon lace. She quickly dressed by candlelight, eager to get to church. Marie was sleeping peacefully. The maid would be nearby if she awoke.

Zélie was the first person to arrive for Mass. She walked over to the Blessed Mother's statue. "Jesus, thank You for sharing Your mama with me. Today I have a very special request for her." She took a little piece of paper and wrote a prayer on it. She carefully dotted her i's and crossed her t's. She was going to make sure what she wanted was very clear. She placed the note at the feet of the statue. "I want another little girl."

Nine months later to the day, Zélie was holding another little girl, Marie-Pauline. She had been born the previous day and baptized. Isidore and Pauline Romet were her godparents. Zélie smiled at Louis and said, "The Blessed Mother interceded!"

Louis grinned at his wife. "Jesus is a good Son; He can't resist His Mother's requests."

Marie loved her baby sister. As the girls grew, it was fun seeing their unique personalities. They both had brown hair and eyes. Marie was independent and talkative at home, but in public she was shy. Pauline was a smart little girl who was quick to understand her parents' words but slow to speak. She was also slow at learning to walk because she was afraid of falling. Pauline was very affectionate—she would blow kisses to Jesus!

~

It was late spring 1863. Marie, three, and Pauline, almost two, were playing in their bedroom. They could hardly contain their excitement when Louis walked into the room. "Papa, can we see our little sister?" Marie asked.

Louis smiled. The previous evening, June 3, 1863, Marie-Léonie had been born! "You may see her when your mama awakes and says, 'Come in.'"

Marie and Pauline waited patiently until they were called. They ran to their mother in bed.

Zélie smiled and moved the blankets so they could see. In her arms lay the little baby, fast asleep, breathing quietly.

"She is a dolly!" Marie whispered. "When can we play with her?"

Zélie chuckled. "When she is older. Right now all Léonie wants to do is sleep and eat."

Pauline blew her little sister a kiss.

That day, the Feast of Corpus Christi, Léonie was baptized. Louis' nephew, Adolphe, and a friend, Madame Léonie Tifenne, were the godparents this time. Louis and Zélie had a tradition of giving their child the name of one of the godparents, thus the name Léonie.

Léonie was very different from her sisters. She had blond hair, blue eyes, and was weak. Zélie and Louis were concerned about her. She was always sick.

Louis and Zélie were very busy; besides taking care of the girls, they had two businesses to run: the clock shop and the lace-making company. Finally, they decided Zélie should stop supplying the company in Paris with lace. Instead, Louis would go to Paris and find buyers for the lace. In this way Zélie would be able to decide how much lace her company would make.

"You will have a chance to check on Isidore while

you are there. His letters don't say much. I worry about him," Zélie said.

"I also worry about him," Louis responded. "He does not have a strong faith to sustain him amid the lure and greed of people. I often shudder to think what would have happened if God had not made me suspicious of some fellow students in Paris. They were trying to trick me into joining their secret society."

"God was not going to let you get caught by them unaware. You wanted to do God's will. Isidore does not have a close relationship with God. I think Isidore wants to be a doctor for fame and money, not to help people. I wish I could do more than just write letters and pray."

"Prayer is worth more than we imagine, Zélie. We must have faith. God doesn't answer all our prayers as easily as He did with your request for Pauline."

"I am learning He often answers our prayers differently than we want."

"That is where faith comes in," Louis told her.

Louis traveled to Paris. He visited Isidore and got orders for Zélie. He went to Our Lady of Victories Church again. The peace and beauty of the church made him think of Heaven. He also visited the Cathedral of Notre-Dame; its restoration was nearly finished. The structure had narrowly escaped being torn down due to its extreme disrepair. Victor Hugo, the famous author, had written a book in 1831 called *The Hunch-*

back of Notre-Dame to raise awareness about the historic building. Louis looked at the tall, ornate ceilings and the incredible stained glass. He thought of how his namesake, Saint Louis, had helped complete the cathedral in the thirteenth century and had paid for two of the rose windows. He also thought of how during the revolution the cathedral had been desecrated; parts of it had been sold, and the nave had been used as a warehouse. *God cares about us so much that He keeps giving us another chance, even with our cathedral.* "Thank You, Lord."

Zélie missed Louis greatly, and every day she hoped it would be the day she would hear from him. Unlike her, Louis was not a writer. He wrote only when he had news to tell.

Finally, a letter came.

Zélie eagerly opened it.

"My dear friend," it started.

Zélie continued reading the letter and realized how much Louis missed them. *He is telling me to stay calm; he knows how hard that is for me*, Zélie reflected. *How wonderful: he found some buyers!*

"Mama, what does it say?" Marie was tugging on Zélie's skirt.

"It says Papa is missing us, that he will be home soon, and that he hopes you and Pauline are being very good."

"We are," Marie said.

I am so blessed to have such a holy and kind husband. He signs it so tenderly: "Your husband and true friend, who loves you for life." *I hope other woman are as fortunate as I am.*

The next week Louis was met at the train station by Zélie, Marie, and Pauline. The little girls wanted hugs; Zélie had to wait her turn. Her face was beaming.

"I missed you so much," Zélie told Louis.

"And I missed you. Being away made me realize how blessed we are."

~

Pauline was quite the character. She was funny and mischievous. Before shepherding the family out the door for church on Good Friday, Zélie gave Pauline a paper doll Élise had sent her. It was of a Visitation Sister. Pauline was very happy with her new toy, and Marie was content with a little prayer book. *Unless Léonie cries, I should have peace during the service*, Zélie thought, relieved.

The Martins found their usual places in Saint Pierre's. Zélie held sleeping Léonie while Louis kept an eye on the other two girls. Soon Zélie was lost in deep thought, meditating on Jesus' Passion and His love for mankind.

It was during a very quiet moment of the service that Zélie heard a rustling next to her. She turned to look at Pauline.

Pauline had stood up. She was holding her paper doll in the air. Waving the paper doll, she shouted, "Here is my aunt!"

Everyone around started laughing, but Zélie cringed. She wanted to sink through the floor!

~

That summer, Zélie and Louis had a new concern. Zélie, who was expecting another baby, had realized with Léonie that she would not be able to nurse again successfully. The new baby would not receive enough nutrition. She had supplemented with the new "remedy," a bottle, for Léonie, but it would not be sufficient on its own. It was a tragedy to think that after her child was born she would have to entrust another woman to care for the baby. Louis, meanwhile, was concerned about the influence another mother might have on their child.

"The wet nurse needs to be not just healthy but also caring and wholesome. The first year is crucial."

"I know. It's time we start some interviews. I am entrusting the problem to God."

They found a good, caring woman who lived on a farm a little distance from Alençon. The woman seemed trustworthy.

On October 13, 1864, Marie-Hélène was born. Zélie was certain little Hélène was the prettiest baby she had ever seen. The Martins tried to see Hélène at the wet nurse's whenever they could. Zélie would often make the trip by herself since she was so eager to go.

Three months after Hélène's birth, Léonie became very ill. Louis and Zélie were at a loss for what to do. The doctor's remedy had not helped at all. Zélie wrote to Isidore for medical advice and to her sister for prayers. Louis made a pilgrimage on foot to pray at the shrine of Notre-Dame de Séez for Léonie. It seemed only a miracle would save her.

Louis returned from the pilgrimage to find his wife cradling their little girl. "She is still not better?" he asked.

"No." Zélie seemed ready to cry. "I keep asking God why He lets her keep suffering. Why won't He heal her?"

Louis sat down next to Zélie and put an arm around her. "It is only natural for us to question such things," he said, looking at her with compassion. "Everyone asks these questions sometime in his life, but as Christians we have answers that others don't. We know how to ask for help and thus receive it. God understands our condition: He made us, and Jesus became man. Even though Jesus was also God and sinless, He still cried at the tomb of Lazarus—even knowing that He was about to raise Lazarus from the dead. We must keep trying to trust God. He has the whole picture in front of Him; we see only a dot."

"You seem to know just what to say."

"I keep saying these things to myself too, so that I might have the faith to move forward. I also recall what my mother once said to a woman after my last sister died."

"What was that?"

"She said, 'I am so grateful to have had my children, even for a short time. Every life is a gift; we cannot take life for granted.' As the English poet Tennyson said, 'It is better to have loved and lost, than never to have loved at all.'"

"Your parents have lost so much, but it has only strengthened them."

"Yes, because they have used their hardships for good and have never given up hope."

"Madame," the maid interrupted, walking into the room, "a letter came from your sister."

"Louis, please read it aloud!"

Louis broke the seal and read the note to Zélie. Élise wrote she was making a novena to a Visitation nun, Blessed Margaret Mary of Alacoque, who had recently been beatified, and Élise was very hopeful for a cure.

"Élise, as always, sounds so faith filled. She gives me strength."

It was at the end of the novena that Léonie suddenly started improving. Each day she grew stronger. Zélie and Louis watched, amazed. All of her health problems from birth disappeared. She was still small in size, but she was growing. Soon she was very strong. Zélie and Louis praised God for the miracle, and they felt indebted to Sister Marie-Dosithée and Blessed Margaret Mary.

The older girls were doing well. Pauline was still lively, but she was better behaved now. She was very funny and sometimes would tease Marie.

"Look, Marie!" Pauline exclaimed, pointing to a portrait of their uncle Isidore. "My godfather is more handsome than yours. Mine has hair on his head, and yours is bald."

~

On Christmas Eve, Louis and Zélie watched Marie, Pauline, and Léonie put their shoes in front of the fireplace. In the morning they would be filled with small gifts and sweets. On New Year's Day, as the local custom went, the children would receive bigger gifts from family members. Zélie thought of little Hélène asleep in her cradle upstairs; she had come home from the wet nurse.

"The children are so excited!" she said to Louis.

"Yes! You know, nine months ago we were not sure Léonie would survive."

"But she did!"

The next morning the girls were in raptures over their Christmas gifts. Zélie, watching them, thought, *I have my gifts too: Louis and my four precious dolls!*

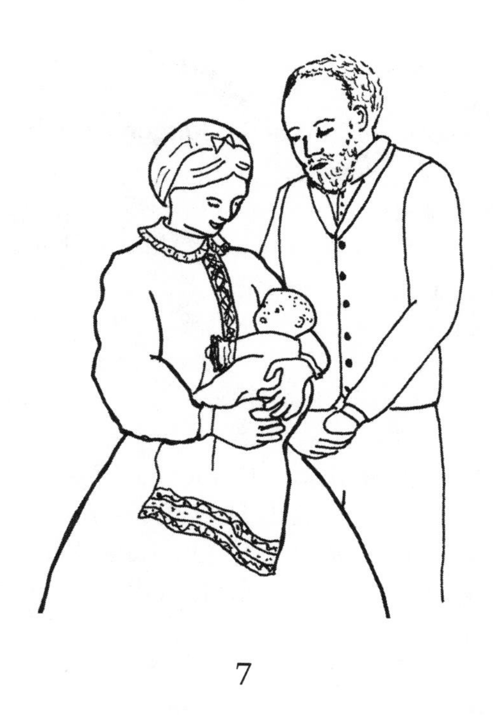

7

THORNS IN THE ROSE GARDEN

LOUIS SAT AT A WORKTABLE in his shop, mending a clock. As he worked he kept thinking about his new baby boy. Even a difficult customer complaining that Louis was not open on Sundays had not disturbed his joy. Politely he had explained that Sunday was the Lord's day; he would not be like everyone else and open his shop. There were six other days of the week to work. Louis was quite used to explaining his actions after all these years, and he no longer thought anything about it.

The shop door opened, and Louis looked up to greet his customer. "Good morning, Vital! What a surprise and a pleasure to see you."

"My clock is not winding properly, and I thought this was the perfect chance to come by and see how your wife and little Joseph are doing," Louis' friend Vital Romet said.

Louis smiled and took the clock. "Zélie is fine, and Joseph is strong and well. He was born on September 20. We were fortunate to find an excellent nurse for him. He is with her now in the village of Semallé."

"You have your little boy!"

"Yes. Zélie and I have so wanted a son. We pray that Marie-Joseph-Louis may be called to the priesthood. Maybe he will get to be what I was not meant to be: a monk."

"Time will tell. I am so glad Isidore is coming to town again. He had his introduction to medicine in my pharmacy."

"Isidore and his bride will be arriving next week. We are having a reception in honor of them. It will be our first party since my father's death. I know you are also planning one, and I am sure several other friends will host parties for them. It will be a busy week. Zélie is very excited to see Isidore and meet Céline."

Zélie could hardly wait to see her brother again. Isidore had decided to become a pharmacist instead of a doctor. He had moved to Lisieux, bought a pharmacy from Monsieur Fournet, and then, several months later, married Monsieur Fournet's daughter Elisa-Céline. Louis and Zélie had been unable to attend the wedding because Joseph was due. The wedding had been September 11, 1866, and Joseph was born only nine days later.

Zélie wondered what Céline would be like. Isidore had been infatuated with a wealthy young lady in Paris whose chief interests had been money, beauty, and pleasure. She would have ruined him. Zélie prayed that Céline would be a good and wholesome woman who would influence Isidore for the better.

Several days later Céline and Isidore arrived at the house. Zélie rushed out to meet them. Céline Guérin emerged from the carriage. She was dressed in a fashionable but tastefully designed dress. Her youthful face was pretty, and she was smiling broadly. Her eyes had a kind, innocent, and joyful look to them.

"Zélie," she said, "I am delighted to meet you. Isidore has talked so much about you."

"It is my pleasure." Zélie felt she and her new sister-in-law would become good friends.

The week was wonderful. It was amazing that fun-loving Isidore had found such a remarkable young lady as Céline.

Monsieur Guérin, who now lived with the Martins, was pleased with his gentle daughter-in-law, and the little girls were enchanted with Uncle Isidore and Aunt

Céline. Zélie and Louis' party was a success, as was Vital's, but the wonderful week was over all too soon, and Isidore and Céline returned to Lisieux.

Whenever Zélie had a chance she would walk the five miles to see little Joseph at the wet nurse's house. Rose and her husband, Moïes, lived on a farm with their three children, one of them near Joseph's age. Joseph was getting big and strong. Never had one of the children been this healthy other than Marie. Zélie was sure someday he would become a priest. She would make his vestments and decorate them with point d'Alençon!

~

It was New Year's Day 1867. Monsieur Guérin had traveled to Lisieux for Christmas and had returned laden with gifts from Isidore and Céline for the children. The family gathered around him and the trunk.

"Grandfather, what is in it?"

"Be patient. I am undoing the latch." Monsieur Guérin opened the suitcase.

"Look! A beautiful doll!"

"A tea set!"

"A new game!"

"A doll trunk and clothes!"

Monsieur Guérin sat down surprised. The girls were shouting joyfully over each new gift. It was as if these girls had no toys!

"See, girls, each gift has someone's name on a tag attached to it," Louis told them. "This game is for Marie. The doll trunk has Pauline's name on it."

Léonie started to sniffle. "I want the doll trunk."

Hélène looked glum. "Me want game; me like playing games."

"Léonie, Hélène, you have presents also. The doll is for you, Léonie, and the tea set is for Hélène. There are still more gifts in the trunk."

"Me want game and tea set."

"I have a doll—I want a trunk!" Léonie exclaimed.

"I like games better than Marie," Pauline added.

"But I want my game!" cried Marie.

Monsieur Guérin stood up and started to pack up the gifts. "If you girls cannot behave and be thankful, I will take away the presents."

"You can't do that," Marie said, "because you didn't give them to us."

"Girls, why are you crying over gifts that you will all play with together?" Louis asked. "The person who is the most sharing will have the most fun."

"I am ready to play the game with you," Zélie added, sitting down at the table. "Hélène, climb on my lap. Léonie, sit next to me. Marie and Pauline, dry your tears and come. Marie, please open the game."

Finally the girls became cheery again. The game was very entertaining, and soon they were laughing.

"Madame Zélie," Louise, the maid, interrupted, "Rose and Joseph are here."

Zélie jumped to her feet. "Bring them in!" She hurried toward the hall followed by Louis and the girls.

"My precious Joseph!" Zélie exclaimed as she held him. "How well you are growing. Rose, sit down and rest. Louise will bring you warm cider. Thank you so much for bringing him here today."

"You're welcome. I must leave, though; some relatives are expecting me. I will return in a couple of hours for him."

After Rose took her leave, Zélie gazed at Joseph. "What beautiful little hands you have. Someday you will be blessing people with them. I have a little hat for you from your aunt and uncle. Let's see how it fits . . . perfect! Aren't you cute." Joseph cooed happily. "I've made you a new outfit. We shall see if it fits you."

Zélie proudly carried Joseph in his new outfit around the house. Madame Martin had to hold him. Then it was time to show him off to Grandfather. Several friends came by to wish the Martins a happy new year. Zélie showed them Joseph dressed like a little prince.

Louis, watching her, commented, "You are treating him like a wooden statue of a saint."

"But he's enjoying it. See, Joseph is laughing!"

All too soon New Year's Day came to a close. Rose took Joseph back with her. The girls were tucked in their beds. Louis retired. Zélie stayed awake to finish an urgent order of lace, then she also climbed into bed.

Louis and Zélie were sound asleep when suddenly they heard a loud banging on their front door. Louis quickly got out of bed, put on a robe, and left to answer it. Zélie put on her dressing gown and slippers. The clock was striking three as she walked into the hall. She heard a man's voice say, "Tell your wife to come quickly. Your little boy is very sick. We are afraid he will die."

Zélie fled back to her room and quickly dressed. *My Joseph . . . die? It couldn't happen.*

Louis hurriedly wrote a note for the maid and then got dressed. A few moments later, he and Zélie left the house.

It was a frigid night, and the icy paths were partly covered by snow. The lantern Louis carried did not give much light, and it made odd shadows around them. "Please, God, spare him," they prayed.

Rose was sitting in her cottage near the fire, holding little Joseph. His face was covered with a rash and was swollen, but he was still alive!

The doctor had already arrived. "This is a bad case of an infection called erysipelas. He is in very grave danger. What did he do today?"

"He came home for a few hours," Zélie said miserably. "I had pleaded with Rose to bring him for New Year's Day."

"He shouldn't have been out in this cold weather. I will do my best."

"And we'll pray," Louis added.

"Louis," Zélie said softly, "God mustn't take him from us now."

Louis put an arm around her. "Let's pray together. God gave him to us. He is God's to call home, but surely God wants to heed our desire to raise Joseph to bring people to Him."

Joseph recovered, but he was no longer a strong little boy. Weak and susceptible, he caught the same illness again and another one at the same time. Rose brought him home to Alençon.

The doctor shook his head. "It is hopeless."

"It is never hopeless," Zélie said, holding her sick baby. "Léonie recovered. Surely God will answer our prayers again."

The doctor shook his head one last time and left. Joseph was rapidly getting worse. Louis and Rose stayed beside Zélie while Louise, the maid, hovered nearby in case she could help. The house was very quiet: Louis had not opened his shop, and Madame Martin had taken the girls away for the day.

"Isn't God going to answer our prayer?" Zélie asked.

No one answered.

It was already dark when Madame Martin brought the four girls home. She dreaded walking into the house, but she knew her son and his wife would need her, and it was after the girls' bedtime. She opened the door of the house. It was silent inside.

Louise met them on the stairs. "Girls, I will help you get ready for bed tonight. Don't disturb your parents."

The girls looked as if they were ready to cry. Madame Martin gave them each a kiss. "Be brave. You will help your mother and father very much if you listen to Louise tonight. Tell her about the fun we had in the park together."

Louise took the girls to their bedrooms, and Madame Martin walked to the parlor. Louis and Zélie were sitting side by side in the dark room, only a lamp casting light on them. They were alone.

"Mother," Louis said, "Joseph . . . died."

Madame Martin started to cry as she put a hand on Louis' shoulder. "I am so sorry." She stood there a moment before giving Zélie a hug. Zélie looked paler than Madame Martin had ever seen her.

"I was so sure God would give us another miracle," Zélie said softly.

"I'm sorry."

"We had such great dreams for our Joseph. I was sure God would answer our prayers for that reason if for no other."

Madame Martin sighed softly. There was so much she could say, but they were not ready to hear it. They would find their strength in God and come to understand that God's ways are beyond human comprehension. They would find peace by their acceptance. Tonight she would say only a little to them. "I was thinking those things when my little Sophie died. She had been healthy for nine years; I was in complete shock and disbelief. It took me a long time to realize that I was so grateful for the short time she was with me and that she never really left me. Joseph is closer to you than you think. We want to plan a perfect life for ourselves on this earth, but God wants it to be in Heaven with Him. Your blessed little Joseph will help you more than you can imagine."

Élise heard the news and immediately started praying for her sister. She knew how hard her sister must be taking it. She sent the Martins a beautiful letter. In it she told how she had been praying after Holy Communion for them and had heard an interior voice say, "I wanted the firstfruits, and I will give you another child who will be what you want."

Zélie read the letter. Whenever she was very sad she had trouble crying, but now she felt tears in her eyes. *We must have faith*, she thought.

"Louis, I am going to pray a novena to Saint Joseph for another boy," Zélie told him. "I will do it in March and have it end on Saint Joseph's feast, March 19."

"I will join you. We could call him Joseph, after Saint Joseph and our little one."

Meanwhile, two-and-a-half-year-old Hélène had developed a persistent earache and was developing a large sore on her ear. She had been taken to several doctors, but no one was able to help her. As it got worse, Hélène lost her hearing in that ear.

One day, Zélie and Hélène were returning from a doctor's appointment. The doctor's verdict was as dismal as ever. "God, please help us find a way to heal Hélène's ear," Zélie prayed. And then she had an idea. *Of course, that is it!* Zélie leaned down to Hélène. "Why don't we say a prayer to our little Joseph and ask him to cure your earache?"

"Yes, please."

Zélie and Hélène walked into Saint Pierre's and knelt down.

Hélène, in her charming way, whispered, "Joseph, fix my ear, please."

Zélie prayed, "Please, dear little Joseph, intercede for us to God. Ask Him to heal Hélène's ear through you."

The next morning, as usual, Zélie was up long before the girls. When Hélène awoke, she toddled to Zélie. "Good morning, my baby," Zélie said.

"Mama, my ear feels good!"

Zélie looked at the ear. It looked fine! All traces of the sore were gone.

Zélie covered Hélène's other ear. "Can you hear me, Hélène?"

"Yes, Mama, very good."

"Joseph has given us a miracle!"

~

On December 19, nine months after Saint Joseph's feast day, the Martins sixth child was born. Marie-Joseph-Jean Baptiste was baptized the same day.

"Saint Joseph is prompt, just like the Blessed Mother was!" Zélie said, cradling her second little Joseph.

All too soon Joseph had to go to Rose's house. Zélie

and Louis resumed their walks to Semallé. He was so much like their first little boy.

"He will be a great priest someday," Zélie happily remarked.

"And hopefully a missionary," Louis added, "to tell people throughout the world how much God loves them."

Meanwhile, Isidore and Céline sent the good news that they had had a baby, a little girl named Jeanne-Marie-Élisa. She would be called Jeanne. Monsieur Guérin traveled to Lisieux to see his new grandchild. Zélie looked forward to the summer when the Martin family would be able to travel.

Summer came. Little Joseph was not well. He came home in July because Rose was caring for her sick mother, and Zélie thought Rose was overburdened. Monsieur Guérin was also ill. Zélie was delighted when Isidore and Céline announced they would visit Alençon. The Martins' trip to Lisieux would wait.

The girls loved their brother. They would happily entertain him.

Eight-year-old Marie would go to his crib. "Naughty little Joseph," she would tease. Joseph would stick out his lower lip, and tears would come into his angelic eyes. Marie would quickly say, "No, no, Joseph is a good boy!" Then Joseph would be all smiles.

Their parents' bed was near the crib. When the girls climbed on it, Joseph could see them. He liked seeing their eager faces.

"Let's jump on the bed!" Pauline declared one day. "Joseph will think it is funny."

Joseph did think it was funny seeing his four sisters bounce up and down. He laughed.

"This is fun!" Hélène exclaimed.

"Jump higher!" Pauline commanded.

Louis and Zélie were both working in nearby rooms. Suddenly they heard a loud crash and crying. They dashed toward their room.

In the crib, Joseph was crying. On what used to be their bed, four little girls were crying. "We broke your bed!" Pauline declared tearfully.

"You certainly did!" Louis replied. "And now you can help me fix it."

~

Joseph continued to get sicker. There was nothing doctors could do to help him. Only a miracle would save him. The Martins prayed fervently, but on August 24, 1868, their second little Joseph also died.

"O God," Louis and Zélie prayed, "must You have allowed his death? Not our will, but Yours be done."

Zélie and Louis did not have much time to grieve. Monsieur Guérin was seriously ill. Isidore came from Lisieux. Monsieur Guérin got worse. On September 3, he died. Once again, Zélie was so sad she could not cry.

~

As the weeks passed, Louis kept thinking about Zélie's health. She was grief stricken and overworked. He tried to help her as best he could. Louis was also concerned about his two older daughters. They were attending a local Catholic school. Although Marie loved to learn, she was scared of the teachers, and Pauline frequently got into trouble with them. Recently Marie had told her parents about the inappropriate behavior of another student. Louis and Zélie were both disturbed. Finally, Louis decided to mention an idea to Zélie.

One evening, when the girls were in bed, Louis knew it was the time. Zélie was sitting at her worktable assembling lace by candlelight. Louis sat down next to her.

"Zélie?"

"Yes, Louis," she said, her fingers working nimbly.

"Well . . ."

"I understand. We have business to discuss." Zélie put down the lace.

"It is about Marie and Pauline. What if we were to send them to Élise's school? We would miss the girls, but they would receive an excellent education. The Visitation Sisters are highly thought of as teachers. And your sister would be there to watch and guide them. She is such a holy witness to Christ."

"The thought has crossed my mind to send them there, but I have always rejected it. After the death of our little boys, it would be so hard to send Marie and Pauline away to Le Mans."

"I know it would be. But we have to think of the

girls: they need a good education. Remember how inspired you were by the religious who taught you—we want the girls to have that atmosphere. There does not seem to be a good school for them in town."

"Louis, I have been realizing that." She sighed. "Maybe we should send them to Le Mans. Let me think and pray about it."

Louis and Zélie prayed and conversed over the next several days. Finally, Zélie also came to the conclusion that it would be for the best to send the girls to Le Mans. She wrote Élise, who said she could help with the girls' admission. Louis and Zélie told Marie and Pauline the plan.

"Mama, Papa, we will miss you so much," Marie said.

"It will be no fun without you," Pauline added.

"Your aunt will be there, and you will make friends with your fellow students. We will come to visit you and write letters. There will be vacations when you can come home," Zélie reassured them. "Pauline, your godmother, Mademoiselle Romet, and her brother, Papa's friend, Monsieur Romet, often go to Le Mans to visit a sibling there. They will visit you also."

"Yes, Mama and Papa," the girls agreed.

~

Zélie took the girls to Le Mans, where Élise and the other sisters gave them a warm welcome. Zélie was sure the girls would start liking school.

At home, Zélie still had her hands full with the little girls and the lace business. Good-natured Léonie was a slow learner. Hélène was charming and smart, but she was not a strong child. And God was giving the Martins another child! Zélie so hoped that this child would live for a long time.

~

On April 28, 1869, a little girl was born. Zélie and Louis named her Marie-Céline. Vital Romet became her godfather, and Aunt Céline was the godmother.

Rose had not been available to care for their little child, so Zélie and Louis had interviewed several wet nurses in Alençon. Within a few days of Céline's birth, the wet nurse chosen proved to be incapable, and the Martins' employed a new one. Louis, however, did not quite trust the woman; he would frequently close his shop to go check on Céline.

One day, a few weeks after Céline had been born, Louis went to visit the little girl. He knocked on the door. No one answered. He knocked again. The house seemed deserted. Louis walked back and forth in front of the house, waiting.

Suddenly he heard a baby cry! The sound was coming from within the house.

He tried the front door. It was unlocked! He walked in and hurried up the stairs.

Céline lay in a cradle crying profusely.

He picked up his little girl. "Don't cry. We'll find your nurse." *She is so small and thin!*

Holding her, he went from room to room in the perfectly kept house. No one was home. Where was the wet nurse? How could she abandon Céline? Maybe the neighbors could tell him something.

Louis went to an adjoining house. He had to shout over Céline's crying to be heard by the woman who answered the door.

"She is out for a drink," the woman responded.

"Out for a drink!" Louis exclaimed indignantly.

He found another neighbor.

"She is always drinking," the man told him.

How dare she do such a thing! "I will take you home, Céline. We will find you a responsible nurse!" Louis carried his child home.

Zélie and Louis had so wanted to keep Céline in Alençon, but they had no choice now. Rose had a friend, Madame Georges, in Semallé, who could be trusted. Louis and Zélie brought Céline to her.

"I will do my best to save her. She is very undernourished!" Madame Georges said gravely.

Thankfully, as the weeks went by, Céline grew stronger and healthier.

~

Meanwhile, Louis and Zélie were excited for nine-year-old Marie. She was going to have her First Holy Communion. Normally, she would have had to wait until she was older, but the sisters believed she was ready, and Sister Marie-Dosithée had tuberculosis again. No one knew how long she would live. Aunt Élise carefully prepared Marie. Zélie sent Marie many letters instructing her for her first foretaste of Heaven.

The Martins traveled to Le Mans for Marie's First Holy Communion. As Zélie knelt in the chapel, she thought, *My little Marie looks like a saint in her white dress and veil. She is so reverent.* "Almighty God, please help her always to be this way!"

Afterward, Marie had something to tell Zélie privately. "Mama, everyone thinks Aunt Élise will die. Jesus wanted to give Himself to me as soon as possible. He had to give them a reason to hasten my First Communion day. Now Aunt Élise will get well! I told Saint Joseph he has to intercede for Aunt Élise's cure. Jesus will listen to Saint Joseph."

"Marie, that is not quite how God works. God knows what is best. We see only a fragment of the picture. In Heaven we will understand God's ways. On earth we ask God to answer our petitions, but ultimately our prayer must be 'Father, not my will be done, but Yours.'"

"I know, but Aunt Élise will get better! To thank Saint Joseph, I will take Josephine as my Confirmation name next year."

Sister Marie-Dosithée recovered. Everyone was shocked except Marie.

~

Hélène, however, was not well. As the year 1869 changed to 1870, there was something increasingly angelic about the five-year-old. In February she caught a cold; then suddenly she was feverish and had trouble breathing.

Hélène, sweet as ever, tried to console her sad mama. Despite having difficulty swallowing, she looked at the broth on the table and asked. "If I drink it, will you love me more?"

"Hélène, I love you so much, I couldn't love you more."

Hélène drank her broth.

She lay in Zélie's arms and gazed at her mama lovingly. "Yes, in a moment I'm going to be cured; yes, soon." She lay her head on Zélie's shoulder. Suddenly her heart stopped beating.

What? No! It can't be! Hélène! My little Hélène! Zélie felt numb with shock. *It is my fault . . . I didn't realize she was this sick!* Louis would be arriving home any minute. How could she tell him their Hélène was dead?

Louis came cheerfully into the house. He was returning from an errand that had gone well, and he had bought a small toy for his sick little girl. Louis stopped—the house was strangely quiet. He hurried to Hélène's room.

Zélie was sitting there, holding Hélène. She was bent over like a statue of the Pietà: Mary holding her dead Son.

"Zélie, what happened? . . . No! . . . My little Hélène!" Louis started to sob. "My little Hélène!"

"And it is my fault! The doctor said he didn't need to come back if she didn't get worse. I didn't realize she was worse!"

Louis dropped on his knees and put an arm around Zélie. He was crying. "It's not your fault. Don't blame yourself."

"I can't help it."

Louis was silent; he had to manage to calm himself somehow. "Zélie, we can find peace only in God." Then he started to cry again.

~

The following weeks were the hardest they had ever endured. Zélie, grief stricken, became very sick. She thought she suffered from what Hélène had. Fortunately, Zélie got better, but she kept reproaching herself for Hélène's death. Louis, meanwhile, was cut to the heart with sadness. Marie and Pauline at school were devastated by the news. Léonie took it especially hard, since she had lost her beloved playmate.

"Louis, you must travel to Le Mans. Marie and Pauline need you. I am recovering," Zélie said, convincing Louis to go.

Marie and Pauline ran to their papa when he arrived. They were crying.

Louis sat down with them, one on each side of him. It was so wonderful to see them, even if all three of them were miserable.

"Papa, why did Hélène die?" Marie asked.

"She got very sick, and her heart stopped beating."

"But why did God let it happen? God answered my prayers for Aunt Élise."

"Yes, God answered your prayer. Sometimes God answers our prayers the way we want them answered. And sometimes God answers our prayers—for He listens to every prayer—the way He wants them answered. He knows what is best and what is best for us.

"God wants us as friends. He wants to walk with us on our journey. Some people have short journeys, and some people have long journeys. Hélène and our little Josephs had short journeys. God desires that we have good journeys, no matter how long or short they are."

"Why doesn't everyone have a good journey?" Marie asked.

"Because for us to be able to love, we must also be able not to love. We call this choice, or free will. To help us, God gives us rules—guiding marks—to help us. When we ignore these rules, we can get hurt, which God never desires. He loves us so much that He Himself came to save us. He loves us so much that He became one of us, for love always wants to become like the beloved."

~

At home, Zélie kept recalling the words of the religious sister who taught a little class that Hélène had attended. "Children like her do not live long. They are ready for Heaven so quickly."

Is she in Heaven? Zélie wondered. *Even though she seemed angelic, she wasn't perfect. Is my little girl in Purgatory?* "God, please have mercy on her. It is my fault she was not prepared to meet You."

Zélie went to stand in front of Louis' statue of Our Lady. "Please, dear Mother, ask God to grant Hélène mercy." She stood gazing at the statue.

Suddenly, she heard a tender, internal voice say, "She is here with me."

"She is there with you, Blessed Mother!" Zélie felt an indescribable joy. She could barely wait for Louis to return home to tell him about Mary's words.

When Louis returned, Zélie ran to tell him of her experience.

He smiled. "We will never be able to comprehend God's love for us in this life. He longs for us far more than we want Him. We are the ones who put a limit on God's mercy."

"Very true," Zélie responded.

"Our life is like a rose garden. It is beautiful, but it has thorns."

"Yes, roses have thorns. And some thorns have roses."

8

WAR!

MAMA, WHAT'S HAPPENING?" Seven-year-old Léonie tugged at Zélie's skirt as she sat writing. "Bells are ringing, and people are running around outside."

"France has declared war on Prussia."

"Why?"

"The countries are mad at each other. Why don't you play with Céline?"

"Is Papa going to fight?"

"Léonie dear, he is too old to be a soldier, but if

he were called, he would willingly respond. Céline is crying because she is teething. Please be a good girl and play with her."

Léonie stood there and sulked. Finally, she turned and left to entertain Céline. Zélie thought of how this war had started: long-standing tensions between Prussia and France had erupted over who was to be heir to the Spanish throne.

Zélie sighed and glanced at her unfinished letter. She had told her sister-in-law all about her girls and her search for a godfather. Louis' cousin, Major Henry Charles de Lacauve, was to have been the godfather for the baby soon to be born, but he was going to war. She was worried for him; plus she needed a new godfather. *So many young men are being drafted—most of Isidore's employees are young men; he will be having a hard time in business. I hope it will not be difficult for him to find new employees, since their second baby will be born soon.* Finally, Zélie managed to collect her thoughts and finish the letter.

That evening, Louis closed his shop and walked to Saint Pierre's. He knelt before the Blessed Sacrament and prayed for his country. *Whenever people concentrate on power, wealth, and pleasure, they bring ruin on themselves,* Louis reflected. *France continuously does it to herself. We never seem to learn. I wish I could help my country in more ways than just by prayer and penance.*

The news from the front was continuously depressing. The French soldiers were ill prepared, and their armies were slow to move. For Zélie and Louis, something else was on their minds: their little child would soon be born! And then Louis would be traveling to Lisieux to be godfather to Isidore and Céline's child. Zélie had had to decline being the godmother because she would need to tend to her own child.

Marie and Pauline came home for their vacation, and then on August 16, 1870, Marie-Melanie-Thérèse Martin was born. Six days later their little cousin Marie-Louise-Hélène Guérin was born. After the experience with Céline's wet nurse, Zélie was determined to try to feed the child herself with a bottle, but after several days it was still not working and Thérèse was sick. Zélie contacted a wet nurse in Alençon of whom she already knew and who had good references. The woman took Thérèse to her house, and Thérèse recovered from her illness.

Meanwhile, events in France were tragic. France had declared war on July 19. Now, only a month later, the French armies were being badly beaten. The city of Metz, not far from Strasbourg, was under siege by the Prussians. On September 1, there was a huge battle at the fortress of Sedan. The following morning, the French emperor, Napoleon III, and 83,000 men were taken prisoner. The people of Paris were outraged and sparked a revolution to which the imperial officials gave no major resistance. A new government, a republic, was formed, but within a few weeks the capital city was besieged by the Prussians. The government had to flee to the city of Tours; the new leader escaped in a hot air balloon.

One day Louis received a battered letter. It had come from enemy lines! Louis opened it quickly. It read, "My good brother, Louis." It was from his cousin Henry! Henry said that he had been wounded at the battle of Privat and was a prisoner of war. Fortunately, he was recovering well from the wound. He sent his greetings to the family and good wishes to the child to whom he had not been able to be the godfather. Louis placed the letter carefully in his desk to keep.

~

A new calamity happened to the Martins—Thérèse got sick again. Ten-year-old Marie, on a visit to the wet nurse's with the maid, had noticed that her littlest sister acted famished when she was being fed: as if she was only being fed when the Martins were present. Marie mentioned her concern to her mother. Zélie, horrified, quickly went to see Thérèse. Finding the child sick from malnourishment, she brought her home, but it was too late. Thérèse could not recover from her illness, and she died on October 8. Each time a child died, it seemed as though that death was the hardest one yet to accept.

Zélie missed little Thérèse so much. She hoped that she would have another little Thérèse. Whenever Zélie said, "My poor little girl," meaning Thérèse, little

Céline would come to her mama to hug her. She was sure her mama meant her.

~

One day in late November, Léonie came to find Zélie.

"Look out the window!" she exclaimed. "What is happening?"

"People are fleeing Alençon because the enemy is nearby. They are taking what they can with them."

"Are we going to leave?"

"No. Papa is helping to defend the town, and we are far better off staying here. Anyway, where would we go?"

"Lisieux, to see Jeanne and Marie."

"You will get to go there some other time."

Léonie left the room. Zélie was in Louis' shop tidying and keeping an eye on things. Louis was worried that scoundrels might take advantage of the upheaval in town to steal. Whenever Zélie was alone in the shop, she would dust. With the war ongoing, lace was not in demand, and she needed to stay occupied.

Léonie reappeared. "Mama, why is everyone burying their treasures?"

"It is because they are afraid the enemy might steal their valuables."

"Will they?"

"They might."

"Did you hide our stuff?"

"Yes, some of it."

"What about my dolls?"

"Trust God to take care of your dolls."

That evening, as every evening, Zélie gathered her children in front of the Blessed Mother statue to say their evening prayers. Zélie had so many prayers on her lips that she did not know where to begin. *Of course, my utmost prayer is for Louis.*

Louis was walking through the forest. Normally he would have heartily enjoyed being under the tall trees and hearing his feet crumpling the dry leaves, but today he was preoccupied with France's problems. He was on his way to help the National Guard, which was monitoring the enemy's moves.

He reached the headquarters, a little clearing where large rocks served as chairs and tables. A tough-looking, rugged man was the captain. He looked up from the makeshift table where he was studying a map.

The man spoke to Louis in a tired voice. "You are assigned to watch this road." The man pointed to a small road on the map. "If you see the enemy, figure out how many there are—then come tell us. Make sure they do not see or hear you."

Louis walked toward the road, using his compass as a guide. Upon finding the road, he positioned himself behind some large bushes and trees. He walked back and forth to stay alert and warm. No one passed on the road except a lone squirrel, who crossed infrequently. Overhead some birds chirped. The November sun dipped low in the sky, and a crisp breeze blew the few remaining leaves downward, adding to the carpet on the dim forest floor. Louis shivered.

Suddenly he heard the sound of dry leaves crackling from footsteps. Louis turned around quickly. Someone was walking in the woods toward him! He saw a figure approaching. Was it a friend or an enemy? Louis concealed himself quietly behind a tree. The footsteps continued coming closer. There was a dense bush next to the tree. *If I crouch down and look through the leaves, I should be able to see without being seen.* Louis quietly knelt down and peered through the bush's foliage. Dusk made it difficult to see anything, but he could discern a man walking toward his hiding place.

"Monsieur Martin?" the man said.

Louis breathed an immense sigh of relief. It was the captain! "Here I am," Louis responded, stepping into the open.

"Sorry for giving you a scare. It's been very quiet here?"

"Yes, there has been no one."

"The enemy has moved on toward Le Mans. You might as well go home."

Louis arrived home around midnight. Zélie awoke as he came in the house, and she eagerly greeted him. "What a relief you are home! They did not need you any longer?"

"No. The enemy has moved on toward Le Mans."

"Oh no! Marie and Pauline are there!"

"Don't worry; we will get them somehow."

The next morning, the maid came bursting through

the door. Louise was very excited as she rushed to Zélie. "A neighbor cannot find the valuables he buried. There are three men digging in his backyard trying to find them. What a tragedy if he loses them!"

"I wonder how long it will take them to find the stuff," Zélie remarked. "Losing one's belongings is unfortunate but certainly not the worst thing that could happen to a person. I am going to the train station to see about a ticket for Le Mans. Don't let the little girls disturb Louis—he is sleeping."

The train station was bustling as Zélie went to the ticket counter. "A ticket for Le Mans, please."

"What are you thinking, lady?" the flustered man responded. "Everyone wants to flee from the fighting! But anyway, I can't help you. The troops have requested the railroad for their own use."

Zélie, with a heavy heart, returned home. Louis was in the shop. She told him her news.

"Since the railroad is unavailable, I will see if I can get to Le Mans by road," Louis said. "I will consult the authorities. Please keep an eye on the shop while I am gone." He put on his bowler hat and frock coat and left the shop.

Marie and Pauline must be so frightened, Zélie thought as she opened her sewing basket. She needed to mend another dress of Léonie's.

"Mama!" Léonie ran into the room. "Louise says dinner is ready and that our neighbor finally found his stuff. It took three men digging all morning to find it. Will that happen to us?"

"No, Louise and I have already taken care of the valuables. Tell Louise to let you children start without me. I need to wait here for your father, or for Louise to replace me after she has eaten."

Louis had only bad news to tell when he returned. "The roads are impassible because of the enemy. The Prussians have been raiding extensively, and the countryside they traveled through is desolate now. One man was trying to prevent a soldier from taking his pig. When the soldier climbed on his horse with the pig, the desperate man clung to the horse's tail. Then the soldier slashed off his horse's tail and galloped away. That is only one of the stories I heard. I will keep trying to get to Le Mans."

The news continued to be grim. There was heavy fighting in Le Mans. Several days later a letter arrived from Sister Marie-Dosithée. Zélie and Louis hurriedly opened it.

"Do not be alarmed or worried," they read. "Marie and Pauline are quite safe here. The Prussians will not enter our convents. A lot of families in town have sent their young daughters to stay at our school during the fighting. Marie and Pauline send their love. They will be sending their letters to you at the next available chance."

Zélie looked at Louis. "We have to trust that God will protect them."

Advent came and then Christmas. It was celebrated quietly this year. Finally, several days later, Zélie was able to travel to Le Mans.

I hardly recognize this place, Zélie thought as she traveled by coach through the city. *There are mobile hospitals everywhere, and everyone seems to be sick! Haven't I seen a Red Cross station on every street?*

It was a great relief to arrive at the Visitation Convent. Zélie rang the bell, and an associate sister opened the door. Zélie was shown to the parlor.

"I will tell Sister Marie-Dosithée and your daughters that you are here," said the associate sister as she left the room.

Suddenly Élise rushed in. "Zélie! I was in the process of writing you when you were announced!"

"I guess you can say what you were writing in person!"

"I will—it was a request for you not to come."

"Why?"

"The municipal authorities just came by to tell us that when the students leave we are going to be sent thirty patients."

"Thirty patients to a cloister?"

"Yes. We already have to house and feed sixteen soldiers in our guest house. We were hoping that if the students remained at school during the break, we might be able to convince the authorities that this is not a suitable hospital. They have already forced the Carmelites to care for thirty patients."

"You know how I long for my girls to be at home."

"I will talk with Reverend Mother," Sister Marie-Dosithée said quietly, before leaving the room.

Zélie sat in the parlor, worried. She dearly looked forward to these breaks, and she knew she would feel better having the girls at home. But the Visitation Sisters had a dilemma. Sister Marie-Dosithée was an associate sister because of her health, so she had more interaction with the outside world. The nuns had chosen and promised to live a cloistered life. To force them to care for servicemen showed a lack of respect for their way of life. Zélie thought of Alençon. *I would prefer that they make me take care of the ill before forcing the Poor Clares in Alençon to do it.*

"Mama!" Pauline rushed into the room. Tears were in her eyes. "Marie is crying. We want to go home," she sniffled, "but we also want to help the sisters. If we leave, will the authorities make all the girls go home, even the ones who have no home to go to anymore?"

"I don't know. Where is Marie?"

"Come." Pauline led her mother into the hall.

At the top of the stairs Marie stood clinging to the banister. She was sobbing. Zélie started up the stairs toward her. She found her daughters' crying contagious, for she also had tears in her eyes. *This is no time to cry*, Zélie told herself. *I must console my girls.*

Sister Marie-Dosithée reappeared. "Zélie, Reverend Mother says take them, but please be quiet and quick about it. Marie and Pauline, I will find you some help for packing your trunks."

Marie and Pauline ran toward their rooms. Sister

Marie-Dosithée and Zélie followed slowly. Zélie wondered when she would see her sister again with the ongoing war.

"Don't expect to bring the girls back for a while," Sister Marie-Dosithée said.

"I intend on keeping the girls at home for the duration of the war. I feel better having them close. Then all I have to worry about is you and Isidore and his family."

"Don't worry; just pray."

"I try not to worry, but it is hard. Who knows what will happen?"

The trunks were packed hastily. A coach was brought to the door, and Zélie and the girls quickly climbed into it. The trunks were placed on top of the carriage. Then the coach rattled over the uneven pavement. There was no grand farewell from the other students or teachers. Zélie felt as if she were a fugitive running away from authorities. *I should be praying that we make the train.*

The coach pulled up to the railroad station. Zélie looked at the clock on the top of the elegant building. "Girls, we have only ten minutes before the train leaves!" Zélie hastily motioned to a porter. "Please take the trunks." She led the way into the station. Pauline had to run to keep up with her mother and Marie.

"We have three tickets for Alençon on the three-forty train," Zélie told the conductor.

"Sorry, madame, the train is full."

"I bought these tickets hours ago! See?" Zélie held out the tickets. "You have to honor your own tickets."

"Everyone wants to leave Le Mans right now. I will see if we can attach another railroad car for you." As he walked away he grumbled, "Next time get here sooner."

"What will happen?" Marie asked.

"I don't know." Zélie spoke worriedly. "We must pray he will honor our tickets."

"They're attaching another car!" Pauline exclaimed.

"They are!" Zélie led her girls and the porter with the trunks toward the empty railroad car.

"Thank You, God!" Zélie prayed silently.

The trunks were placed in the car, and Zélie thanked the porter. Then the conductor helped her and the girls into the empty car. A moment later the train was leaving the station.

"What a blessing this is," Zélie commented. "We have a whole car to ourselves!"

Upon their arrival home, Louis and the little girls greeted them enthusiastically. That night the girls all went to bed happy; Louis and Zélie, however, stayed up late, talking. Louis had to hear about the sad situation in Le Mans.

"I realized we have experienced nothing when I saw Le Mans. I am so glad we are almost finished with this unfortunate year. I hope 1871 is better."

"I hope so too."

New Year's Day 1871 came quietly. Louis and Zélie were very thankful the family was all together. As the days passed, the news from the front was disastrous. For two days the battle of Le Mans was fought. The

French were defeated on Thursday, January 12. Rumors spread rapidly that Alençon was the next city to be attacked. Friday came and went slowly. People were hiding their valuables again and fleeing town. Saturday passed with fear and dread.

On Sunday morning Zélie arose early and attended the first Mass because Céline was sick. Zélie would stay home with her while the rest of the family and Madame Martin attended a later Mass. Normally the streets were quiet at this hour, but not today. She hurried toward Saint Pierre's.

Several hours later Louis, Madame Martin, and the three older girls walked to Mass. The streets were thronged with refugees.

"Papa, what's happening?" Pauline wanted to know. "Who are all these men?"

"They are the National Guard. Last night they assembled in town. We must pray."

Madame Martin sighed. "When will France ever learn? We must look for our strength in God."

That morning at Mass everyone was earnestly petitioning God to spare their men and the town. Louis thought sadly of all the killed and wounded men and of the many beautiful places to which he had been that were now devastated by war and in enemy hands. "God, please help us," he prayed.

After Mass a petition was passed around outside the church. People were talking loudly and angrily. Louis read the petition and signed it. *The situation is very dangerous. We must get home immediately.*

Louis hurried his family home. He quickly found Zélie in Céline's room. "Zélie, the prefect has given orders to blow up the bridges in town!"

"What!"

"Yes, the bridges will be blown up unless our petition can stop it! We must get everyone into the cellar, and everything we might need."

Zélie groaned. "We live right next to a bridge!"

Louis collected the precious business and family papers and deposited them in a corner of the cellar. Zélie ran around giving directions to the three older girls to bring clothing, books, and toys downstairs. Meanwhile, Zélie was also trying to pack all that she and little Céline might need.

Louis carried Céline to the cellar. He made a comfortable bed for her out of an old trunk and blankets. Then he left her with Madame Martin, who had already brought her necessities neatly packed to the basement.

The girls wanted to bring so much with them to the basement that Zélie had to say, "If you bring all of that downstairs, there will be no room for us."

Once his whole family was safely in the cellar, Louis left the house to learn the news. In the distance was the sound of cannons and guns. *Our poor men are so ill equipped for fighting. I wish I could help them more. It is good for my family that I am too old to be drafted; if I were a bachelor, I would enlist in the Francs-tireurs, the guerrilla force of armed civilians.*

Louis returned home shortly thereafter to inform his family the petition had worked! "The bridges will not be destroyed, but you had all better remain in the cellar. As you can hear, the fighting is not far away from Alençon."

All day they could hear the cannons. The girls cried every time they heard a loud explosion. Zélie kept praying for the soldiers.

At six o'clock in the evening, it was suddenly quiet. Zélie sighed. "Surely it means defeat."

"I will go upstairs to see what happened," Louis said.

Zélie patiently waited until he called them. "Zélie, Mother, come."

Zélie and Madame Martin joined him at the top of the stairs. Louis lowered his voice. "Our soldiers are returning; they have given up. I can see a nearby storefront smashed and shrapnel on our street. Thankfully, our house seems fine."

Zélie looked outside at the poor soldiers walking on the street or being carried on stretchers. There were so many wounded men. Down the street she saw one of the mobile hospitals. *This is so tragic,* she thought. She dared utter what they were all thinking: "What will happen to France?"

9

INVADERS

EARLY THE NEXT MORNING Zélie was again watching soldiers march by, but now they were Prussians! They were an ominous sight with their black flags and a skull design on their helmets. Zélie shuddered. She turned to her mother-in-law, who was standing next to her. "How can people not see that war is a punishment for the way we have acted?"

"People prefer not to look. It is easier to keep doing and defending what one is doing than to admit that our actions do have consequences. We bring war upon ourselves inadvertently."

Louis was downstairs in the shop, guarding his wares. He wandered from thing to thing in the room, trying to focus and avoiding the windows. He felt helpless seeing his country in enemy hands. *I should be praying for my country, but I cannot concentrate. There must be thousands of Prussians here.*

At one o'clock, the parade of soldiers finally stopped. They had been passing in front of the house for six hours. *Now is just the beginning of my vigilance*, Louis thought sadly. *I won't be able to sell my shop to Adolphe if I have no shop. It would be so nice for Zélie and me to have only one business, but will that ever happen?*

A soldier walked by and looked through the window with curiosity. Louis did not let his gaze falter from the man. The Prussian walked on. *I wish I could conceal the expensive clock-making supplies.*

Bang! Bang! Bang! There was loud knocking on the door of the Martins' house. Louis went to answer it, assuming that only the enemy would knock that obnoxiously.

Upstairs, Zélie inwardly groaned. *Oh no, what's happening now?*

Bang! Bang! The knocker sounded impatient.

Zélie looked at her frightened daughters. "I'll go answer it," she said, trying to sound calm.

She met Louis in the hall coming from the shop. "I can get it," he said quietly.

"Are you sure? You do not look well; I will answer it."

Louis did not argue, but he followed her. Zélie opened the door to a Prussian sergeant filling the doorway. In broken French he demanded to inspect the house.

Zélie stood as tall as she could. "Come in," she said to the sergeant. She led the way upstairs to the Martins' living space.

Louis watched her and marveled. *Zélie is able to present such a calm face even in times of trial. The sergeant will be more polite to her than to me. I had better watch my shop.*

"My husband and I live here with our four children, one of whom is very sick; my husband's mother; and our maid," Zélie told the man.

For once, Zélie was glad her daughters had made a mess in the sitting room. Their new toys from Aunt Céline for New Year's were strewn across the floor. Marie was hiding behind a chair, and Pauline and Léonie were staring at the enemy soldier.

The sergeant walked through the rooms on that floor. He made some marks in his notebook. "*Gut,*" he said in German, then walked down the stairs.

Zélie followed him until he had left the house. After the Prussian's departure, Louis joined her. Zélie smiled at Louis.

"What happened?" he asked.

"He didn't like steps, so he never found out that your mother has the whole top floor to herself!"

"Good! There will be one place without them."

A little later Louis was looking out his store windows again. A soldier was walking along the street putting numbers on doors. *Why? . . . Oh, I know what they are doing.*

Zélie came into the shop. "What is happening across the street?"

"They are marking the doors with how many soldiers our neighbors are expected to house." Louis read aloud the numbers: "Fifteen, twenty, twenty-five."

Zélie sighed. "I wonder how many they will assign to us."

"They just wrote on our door!" Louis and Zélie went to open it.

Louis stepped outside. "Nine!" he exclaimed.

"Only nine? We can't complain, but where are we going to house them?"

The next several hours were crazy. Louis, Zélie, and Louise moved beds and carried clothing to the ground floor; there were rooms behind the shop where the Martins would temporarily live. The older girls offered to help.

"Stay with Céline—that will be the most useful thing you can do," Zélie told them. *I don't need a repeat of yesterday's exodus of belongings, just after we finally got it all put away.*

They were far from finished when there was a knock on the front door. Louis opened it. Nine soldiers walked into the hall. Louis felt squashed behind the door.

"Wo sind die Zimmer?" one of them asked.

It was in a different dialect of German than Louis was used to, but he knew what the soldier had said. He wanted to be taken to the rooms. Louis silently led them up the stairs.

"Here," he said in French as he showed them the rooms.

"Wir sind hungrig," one of them told Zélie who was standing in a doorway. *"Fleisch, Heringssalat."*

Zélie gave him a blank face and looked toward Louis. He said nothing.

Another soldier stepped forward and explained in broken French that they were hungry. They wanted meat and herring salad.

"I do not know how to make herring salad," Zélie responded calmly, "and with a war going on, it is hard to get provisions. You will have to settle for mutton stew and bread tonight." She headed to the kitchen, where Louise was already working.

When Louis joined them after dinner in the kitchen, Zélie inquired why he had not translated for her.

"At this point I do not want them to know that I can understand them. I am going to sleep behind the counter in the store. If anyone breaks into the store, I will be able to stop him."

"Good," Zélie said. "So far it seems that our nine are

only eaters, not looters as well. You should have seen the way they ate. They swallowed the mutton stew as if it were soup, and they ate everything without bread. I told them they were going to have to supply the meat tomorrow. I didn't think nine people could eat that much."

Morning came. It was Tuesday, January 17. It already seemed like Sunday had been a week ago, not the day before yesterday. Louis reported to Zélie that there had been no looters during the night. He looked like he had not slept at all, and he had no appetite for breakfast. Zélie sighed; it was going to be a long, distressing day.

This morning the soldiers wanted cheese. Zélie had never seen so much cheese eaten without bread. Meanwhile, she was trying to prepare her children's breakfast, and there was no fresh milk in town. Zélie hurried from the kitchen to the dining room to the girls. She felt as if she had done a day's worth of work, and it was not even nine o'clock!

Louis had given Marie and Pauline a table in the shop to use. After breakfast they started coloring pictures with paints from their aunt Céline. Little Céline was better; she was happily playing with a new doll from her aunt. Léonie joined her.

Louis left the girls to keep watch so that he could go help an elderly neighbor cover his smashed window. Then he made a visit to church. He felt listless and depressed. "God, please send France a miracle to save us. Blessed Mother, please intercede with God for us." Louis returned home to find Zélie in the kitchen cooking.

"The soldiers brought enough meat for thirty people with normal appetites. It was a struggle figuring out how to cook it all," Zélie complained, motioning to an array of stuffed pots in front of her.

"The Prussians have threatened to pillage Alençon if the town does not pay an enormous amount of money," Louis informed Zélie.

"How dreadful!" Zélie's anxiety showed in her face. The prospect of such an occurrence was terrifying. "Why?"

"It is because of our resistance to them."

"What did the mayor say?"

"He refused to pay the amount. Instead he said, 'Might is right. Here are the keys to my house.'"

"What is going to happen?"

"The Duke of Mecklenburg, who is in charge of the Prussians here, was apparently impressed with the mayor's attitude and did not take the keys; however, the whole area has been raided for livestock."

"I know; we had no milk this morning. I don't know what Céline will do without it, and I worry about all the other mothers with young children."

"The telegraph lines have been cut to Le Mans. There is no way to hear from your sister. However, you should be able to send a letter to Lisieux if you do it right now."

"I wonder if Lisieux is experiencing the same horrors that we are. I will write to Céline today. Do you know where the Prussians are heading?"

"The rumor is Laval. If they conquer that city—and it will be a miracle if they don't—Brittany will be an easy victory for them also." Louis sadly sat down at the kitchen table.

"Louis, do you need to eat something?"

"I have no appetite. I will try to rest. Then maybe I will be able to eat." Louis left the room.

Zélie sighed. *Louis is going to make himself sick over his grief!*

"Mama!" Pauline ran into the room crying.

"What is it, Pauline?"

"I lost the brushes, and my picture looks dreadful. Marie is crying too. She says the paints are hers, but I know Auntie said I could use them too!"

"Louise, could you please keep an eye on the meat?" Zélie said to the maid. "I will be back."

Marie was sitting sadly at the art table, sniffling. "Pauline is ruining my paints, and I don't have a brush anymore."

"See, my picture is ruined," Pauline sobbed.

Pauline's picture certainly looked dreadful. She had put every color on it, and all the bright colors had run together to make a dull brown. Zélie could not figure out what the painting was even meant to be. Marie's picture was of swans on a river surrounded by farmland. It was a nice picture, but it was being ruined by her tears!

"You need to go wash your faces. I am taking the paints for now. Aunt Céline meant you both to use them responsibly. Your papa will give you lessons on how to use them. When you look better, come join me in the kitchen. You will feel better doing something else."

When evening fell, it was none too soon for Zélie. *It seemed this day would never end*, she thought. *The children are asleep; Louis is in the shop; I finally have time to write.* Zélie got a piece of paper and her writing supplies. She sat down at a table with her lamp. *If I told Céline everything, it would fill a book.* It was a relief to put down her thoughts. *I am probably terrifying Céline with this account. It is hard to believe unless it has happened to you.* "Please, God, spare others from this calamity." She finished the letter and sealed it. Louis would mail the letter tomorrow.

Zélie knelt and said her night prayers. Surely her heavenly Father was listening to her. He would allow only as much to happen as she could bear. *Someday this war will be over.* "Please, Blessed Mother, ask God for it to be soon."

Louis was lying on his makeshift bed in the shop. He could not sleep. He was fervently praying that Heaven would intercede on behalf of his country.

The next morning nothing seemed different from

the day before: Zélie and Louise cooked; Louis watched the shop; the girls studied and played; and the soldiers still had enormous appetites. At least the Prussian army had now said they would not raid homes and stores.

"Only eat our food," Zélie said wearily.

After the morning meal, she cleared the table of the soldiers' dishes. One of the soldiers looked younger than his companions. He always smiled a thank-you after receiving the food, unlike the others. This morning he walked over to her and timidly said, "Merci." Zélie smiled back at him. Then she carried the plates to the kitchen.

Upon her return to the table she saw most of the soldiers in the sitting room. Some of them were lounging in chairs for a moment, but the young soldier was looking at the photographs of the children on the desk and holding a letter he had received. *He must be homesick.* Zélie recalled how he had nicely stepped aside to let Marie and Pauline pass by him and held open the kitchen door for the girls while they had set the table the previous evening. *He probably has little sisters at home. I will give him some of those pastries and chocolates that I have for the girls. It might brighten his day.*

Zélie gave a little plate of pastries and chocolates to Pauline. "Give this to the young soldier named Hans: he has blond hair, blue eyes, and no beard."

"I know whom you mean. He is the nice one who opened the door for us, the only nice one."

The young soldier was alone in the parlor now. Pauline walked up to him and handed him the plate.

His face broke into a big smile. *"Merci!"* He took the plate, and with his other hand he motioned toward the Martin children's pictures, himself, and his letter.

Pauline nodded. She understood: the letter was from his family.

Using hand gestures, the soldier explained that he had a brother and two sisters at home. One of the girls was Pauline's size. "Paula," he said.

Pauline pointed at herself. "Pauline!" she exclaimed.

They both grinned.

She motioned that she had a sister taller than she: "Marie." Pauline put her hand at her shoulder and said, "Léonie." Then she put her hand not far from the ground and said "Céline."

The soldier nodded his head; he understood.

Pauline walked over to the desk. She picked up a photo of Hélène. "Hélène," she said, and shook her head sadly. She pointed at the pictures of her brothers. "Joseph and Joseph, *non*." She held her arms as if rocking a baby. "Thérèse, *non*," she said, and then shook her head again.

The soldier smiled sympathetically.

"*Bon*?" Pauline grinned at the soldier and motioned for him to try the sweets.

He put one of the chocolates in his mouth. "*Gut*, uh, *bon*?"

"*Bon*!" Pauline smiled and left to find her mother.

Zélie was still in the kitchen, her hands covered in flour as she kneaded dough. "Yes, Pauline?"

"He likes them a lot—he said '*Merci*' and '*Bon*.' He has a brother and two sisters, and one of his sisters is about my age. Guess what her name is."

"I don't know."

"Please?"

"Maria."

"No."

"Anna."

"No. Should I tell you?"

"Yes."

"Paula. Isn't that amazing!"

"Yes."

Meanwhile, Louis had walked upstairs to see Madame Martin. His mother was calmer over the enemy than he was. He was glad that neither his father nor Zélie's father had had to live through this humiliation for France.

Madame Martin was knitting socks by the window. She had a reassuring smile when he entered. "Louis, stop making yourself sick over this. Zélie is worried about you."

"It is so hard to stand by and see France destroyed. What can I do?"

"Pray. This has happened before and will surely happen again if people do not follow God's commandments."

"We never seem to learn."

"Think of the days of Joan of Arc. God sent her to save France, even though the French leaders were cowards."

"Maybe we need another Joan of Arc."

"Help comes in many forms. Right now this war might make people realize that they are not as strong and invincible as they think they are. Maybe it will be a wake-up call to find God."

"I hope so."

"Why don't you take my clock and fix it. It is running slow."

Louis picked up the clock and started down the stairs. He was almost at his shop when he heard noises from within it. *It is probably the girls.* He opened the door and looked. In the corner, half-hidden by shadows, a Prussian soldier stood. He had been in the process of picking up one of Louis' most expensive watches.

The soldier stared at Louis a moment, before speaking. *"Das ist meine Uhr."* He started to walk toward the door with the watch.

Louis ran to the front door and blocked the exit. In excellent German he said, "No, it is not your watch. Put it down and don't ever steal again."

The soldier was taken aback to hear his language spoken so well and with such authority.

Louis repeated, "Put it down."

The man hesitated. Then he put the watch on the counter. Louis stepped aside and let the man leave.

Louis watched him walk down the street. It had been

one of the soldiers stationed in their home, the one called Konrad by his companions. Louis put on his bowler hat and frock coat. He was going to complain to the authorities, but first he had to tell Zélie. Léonie was in an adjoining room. He sent her to find her mother.

Zélie was still in the kitchen, cutting apples with Louise. Léonie ran into the room.

"Mama, Papa wants you immediately in the shop. Something is wrong!"

Zélie put down her paring knife and hurried toward the shop. "Louis, what happened?" she asked as she entered.

"One of the soldiers quartered here was trying to steal a watch."

"Oh no!"

"I am going to report him to the authorities. The duke said they would not steal such things. Will you stay here in the store while I am gone? I was getting laxer with the shop, and I almost paid for it."

"Yes, of course, Louis. I hope you are successful."

Louis left his shop. Few inhabitants of Alençon were in the streets. Prussian soldiers were everywhere: they were eating, drinking, walking, lounging, and doing drills. Louis did not think he had ever seen this many soldiers in one town, not even in the days when his father had been an officer. He rehearsed to himself what he would say; he had not carried on a substantial conversation in German for years, and he wanted to make sure there would be no misunderstandings.

Here it is. Louis looked at the Prussian headquarters. The beautiful Alençon building had the enemy's flag hanging from a pole. Sentries were patrolling it. Louis went to the guard at the front door.

"I request to see the person in charge of the soldiers," Louis said in German.

"*Ja*," the soldier responded, calling another soldier.

The second soldier led Louis into the building. Louis was left to wait in a room. He sat down and looked around. In the doorway a soldier stood guard, but no one else was in the room. The walls still had the portraits of famous Frenchmen, but a Prussian flag covered the painting of Napoleon III. Louis sighed. *It is so hard to see the Prussian flag flying over my land. Will France ever be its own country again? How many more men will die? How will this meeting go?*

A soldier came into the room. "*Kommen Sie*," he said.

The soldier led Louis into a room where an officer was seated behind a desk. The man looked up from his papers. "What is the problem?" he said hesitantly in French.

"I am here to report an attempted theft in my store from one of the soldiers stationed at my house," Louis said in German.

The officer was surprised and relieved to hear his

language spoken. He made some notes and said the intruder would be removed and punished.

Louis was escorted to the street by a soldier. He headed home feeling very relieved. Three soldiers crossed in front of him, one being escorted with his hands tied behind his back and his head bowed in shame. Louis thought of the soldier he had reported, and he hoped his punishment would not be harsh. *I just want Konrad to learn his lesson.*

Louis opened the door of his house. He could hear the soldiers upstairs walking around in their heavy boots. The children were playing in a back room; their voices were lively. *Where is Zélie?*

Pauline ran into the hall. "Papa, Mama wants you!"

"Is she in the shop?"

"No, Grandmother is in there. Mama is in the kitchen."

Louis hurried to the kitchen.

Zélie was sitting at the kitchen table with a newspaper in her hands. She looked very excited. "Louis, have you heard the news?"

"No. What news?"

"Several children just saw the Blessed Mother!"

"Really! Where? When?"

"In the little town of Pontmain, near Laval, last night. Here." Zélie handed him the newspaper. "Read it! The town was going to be invaded by the Prussians, and then the Prussians turned back!"

Louis eagerly took the newspaper and read how seven children had seen a beautiful lady in a dark blue dress covered with stars, standing in the sky. None of the adults praying there had been able to see her. There had been a white scroll in the sky that had said, "But pray, my children. God will soon hear you. My Son allows Himself to be moved with compassion." It was that evening that the Prussians, for some unknown reason, had halted their advance.

Wow! He continued reading how the Lady had moved her fingers in time to the music of a recently composed hymn called "Mother of Hope." *What a sign that is! She must want to be called Mother of Hope!* Then she was holding a red crucifix with the Lord's name on the crossbar: Jesus Christ. *She keeps trying to lead us to her Son!* After that, small white crosses on her shoulder took the place of the large red cross. *She is reminding us we all must carry our crosses with Jesus.* Finally she left, but a mysterious white cloud appeared, hovering over the praying crowd. The bishop of Laval was investigating the events.

Louis laid the paper down. "God is helping us! We have our own little miracle to be grateful for too. The officer listened to my complaint. That soldier will not be sent back here."

"Good!" Before Zélie could respond further, Pauline ran into the room. "Mama, the soldiers say it is dinnertime!"

Zélie smiled. "We still have our crosses to bear!" She walked to the stove.

Louis sat at the table thinking. He kept recalling the

arrested soldier he had seen walking and the soldier on whom he had reported. *France isn't the only one in need of help.*

Early the next morning, Louis went to Mass. Normally, Zélie and he attended daily Mass together; today she was staying in the shop so that he could go.

After Mass Louis talked with Vital; they discussed the recent apparition, and then Louis told him about the attempted theft. "I hope the soldier learns his lesson."

"I think he will. I heard yesterday how a Prussian soldier had stolen eggs and was court-martialed and shot."

"Oh no! Such an extreme punishment never occurred to me! I must take back my complaint immediately. Vital, please stop by my house and tell Zélie that I have gone to talk to the Prussian authorities. And tell her to pray."

Louis hurried back to the Prussian headquarters. He felt dreadful—a man might die because of his accusation. "God, please let it not be too late!"

Once again Louis spoke with a guard, was escorted inside by another soldier, and was left to wait in a room. *Will I be too late? Will they accept my request?* Louis sat down and pulled out his rosary. *Of course, why did I not think of it? I will ask Our Lady, under the title Mother of Hope, to help the soldier! She is not just for France—she is Mother of us all! I really need her, and so does Konrad.*

It seemed an hour had passed, though his pocket

watch said it had been only a quarter of an hour, when a soldier came in and told Louis to follow him. Louis was led through the now-familiar hall to the room he had been in yesterday. The same officer looked up at him as he entered.

"Yes?" This time the officer spoke in German. "What is your complaint now?"

"No complaint. I am here to withdraw yesterday's accusation."

"What?"

"I am here to withdraw yesterday's complaint."

"Why?"

"I am embarrassed to admit that I was overly hasty in assuming that the soldier was stealing the watch. He was looking at the watch, and I thought I saw him try to put it in his pocket. But I might have been mistaken. He was staying in my house, so it would only be natural for him to be in a variety of rooms and to admire things. He did not actually take it away with him, so he should not be convicted of stealing it. Please don't court-martial him and shoot him. There is no complaint against him anymore."

"It is rare to see a French man pleading for a Prussian. All right, you retract your complaint." The officer turned to his assistant. "Send the orders to release the man from custody. There is no longer a case against him." He looked back at Louis. "He will be sent to stay elsewhere. Anything else?"

"No. Thank you very much!" Louis left quickly.

Louis, very eager to tell Zélie what had happened, hurried toward home. The soldier would not be shot! He recalled the Lady's words: "God will soon hear you." *Doesn't that mean the war will end soon?* For the first time in months, Louis felt lighthearted.

From a window, Zélie saw Louis coming and went to meet him. "You were successful!" she exclaimed. "Your face betrays your joy."

"Yes! Zélie, I asked our Mother of Hope to help, and she did!"

10

THE LITTLEST FLOWER

THE WAR WAS OVER! On January 28, after one last unsuccessful battle for the French, an armistice was signed. In May the Treaty of Frankfurt formally ended the war, but in Paris fighting broke out. Many priests and the archbishop of Paris were killed. Concurrently, the stock market collapsed, resulting in an economic depression. In July Louis sold the house and clock shop to Adolphe, his nephew, who had recently inherited a substantial fortune. Madame Martin was still occupying her apartment on the top floor, while the rest of the Martins were living in the childhood home of Zélie, which Monsieur Guérin had left to her. Louis was relieved that he would be able to work full-time helping Zélie with the lace business. Originally the Martins had hoped to buy a bigger house with a large garden for the girls; however, so much had been damaged by the war that there were no other houses available. Now they would attend Zélie's old parish, Notre-Dame, where Zélie and Louis had been married.

I am so tired today, Zélie thought as she boarded a train to Le Mans. The girls had returned to school in April, and Léonie had joined them in June. Today, the first of August, she was picking them up for their summer vacation. It had been such a busy week moving all the furniture. Louis had made sure the furniture was placed just as she desired it. *What a homey house it is. I can't wait to see the girls' expressions when they see the rooms.*

The girls were ready and waiting when Zélie arrived. They were very eager to start their two-month vacation, but Zélie told them she needed some time to visit with her sister. They had many things to discuss.

Sister Marie-Dosithée was not optimistic about Léonie's continuation at the school. "Reverend Mother is not sure we can handle her. I have had to tutor her privately because she was interrupting the class and was unable to comprehend the lessons. Reverend Mother does not want me to keep tutoring her."

Zélie knew why the mother superior did not want Sister Marie-Dosithée to teach Léonie: her health was not up to handling a difficult child. "I understand. I will find a new teacher in Alençon."

"When she is a little older, bring her back here."

Zélie and her girls departed with many friendly good-byes ringing in their ears. *This is so different from last time*, she recalled, *when we felt like fugitives!*

When the girls saw their new home, they were delighted with the rooms. They ran from the sitting room, which would also serve as Zélie's office, to the dining room, to the kitchen. On the next floor, they saw the guest room, Marie and Pauline's room, and their parents' room. The top floor contained a room for Léonie and Céline and a room for Louise, the maid.

"It is wonderful," Pauline declared, "and so quaint!"

"When will Louise return?" Marie asked her mother.

"Once she is well. She has been ill for a month. I cared for her night and day for three weeks; she was barely able to move. Last week we were able to transport her on a bed in a carriage to her home. Her mother will care for her until she recovers. Temporarily we have a cleaning woman who comes during the day."

"Maybe she won't get well," Léonie said hopefully. "Can we see the garden now?"

Zélie looked at Léonie with surprise. "Yes, let's go to the garden."

As Zélie accompanied them down the stairs, she thought of how hard it was to acquire reliable servants.

Zélie always treated servants like family, which people told her was the wrong way of doing things. Last time Louise was ill, Zélie had hired another maid, who had stolen from them. *Louise is like us; she is not perfect, but she means well and is trustworthy.*

Zélie and the girls entered the walkway from the kitchen. It went past the annex, a building Monsieur Guérin had built that connected to the house. It contained a laundry room with a room above it. The walkway ended in a beautiful but small garden. Flowers bloomed profusely in between fruit trees. A vine trellised the high garden walls.

"It's beautiful!" the girls all exclaimed.

I just wish it were bigger. If my father had added another floor to the house as he had intended, and not built the annex, this place would be perfect, Zélie thought. *Oh well, I must remember this is not Heaven and be grateful for what we have.*

Even though the war had wrecked the economy temporarily, rich women still wanted point d'Alençon on their dresses. As commerce picked up, the orders for lace increased dramatically. Louis took care of the finances and made the prickings for the designs. Thus he still got to do intricate and artistic work. He and Zélie always made sure the workers were paid very promptly for their labor, since many of them depended on the money for necessities. If one of the lace makers was sick, Zélie would visit the worker on Sunday and bring gifts.

Life settled into a routine at the new house. Louise

got well and returned. School resumed for Marie and Pauline. Léonie tried another school in Alençon. Céline was often ill, but surviving. The new house had become home.

One rainy day Louis went out on errands. He walked along his street quickly toward home. Their side of the street had homes, but across from them was a magnificent government building, the prefecture. Several of the employees for the city and their families lived in the building. The Martins were good friends with one of the families, the Tessiers. Louis glanced toward the prefecture. Huddled under its porch stood a family. Louis went over to them.

"Good day. Are you all right?" Louis asked.

The father—his once-nice suit now threadbare—responded, "My wife, son, and I were just turned out of our apartment because we could not pay the rent. I lost my job due to the war and am unemployed. We are just staying here until the rain stops."

Louis looked at the boy. He was thin and pale. "Why don't you all come over to my house and have something to eat. My wife is an excellent cook."

"No, no; we mustn't disturb your family," the man said.

"We don't want to inconvenience anyone," the wife added.

"I will ask my wife what she thinks. I will return." Louis hurried across the street in the pouring rain.

He knew exactly what Zélie would say. She always

said the same thing to anyone who needed help: "Of course, bring them here." Just the other day she had decided to shelter and feed a cat that Louise detested. "He's hungry," she had said.

Zélie, upon hearing of the family, insisted on going out in the rain herself to invite them in. Soon she had them sitting near the stove warming themselves while Louise ladled hot soup into bowls for them. While Louis conversed with the father as the family ate, Zélie packed the family a basket of food.

After the family had departed, Louis told Zélie that he was going to try to find the man a job. "I gave them a handful of francs and suggested a cheap place to stay. They felt awkward accepting, so I told them they can return the money when the father has a decent job and they have a roof over their heads. I will talk with my friends to see if I can find him suitable employment."

Louis was successful in finding the man a well-paying job, and the family was very grateful. They were soon able to rent an apartment again. "How can we ever thank you?" they asked Louis.

"It's simple: say thank you to God, and pray for my family and me; that is the type of thanks we like."

The months passed, and 1871 became 1872. As spring and summer rolled by, Zélie became very excited. There was a new little person coming to live in the house. Zélie had been sure Thérèse had been her last child because of her age—at forty, she was old enough to be a grandmother—and she was very happy that it was not true. Her "little one" would be coming around New Year's. *A perfect New Year's gift*, Zélie thought. She so hoped this child would live. *I want a little Thérèse or a little Joseph whom I get to keep.*

As the weeks and months went by, Zélie was certain that this child was different from the others. When Zélie sang, her little one seemed to sing with her. This child seemed stronger.

One evening Zélie decided to stay downstairs after everyone else had retired for the night; she wanted to finish the chapter she was reading about a saint. Afterward she closed the book and thought about the saints. Some of them had supernatural experiences, and some of them actually struggled with the devil physically. *I am so glad I do not have their temptations.*

Suddenly Zélie felt terrifying hands clutching her back. She turned, but there was no one there.

"Jesus, help me!" She frantically made the sign of the cross.

The thing was gone as suddenly as it had come.

After a few seconds of shock, Zélie was able to breathe a huge sigh of relief. "Please, God, protect me as You have always protected me from the snares of the devil." Then she hurried upstairs to her bedroom. She did not want any more supernatural experiences that evening.

~

Sister Marie-Dosithée was quite excited over the little one. She wrote Zélie a long letter. Zélie, as always, was delighted to get correspondence from her sister. She opened it promptly.

"Mama, are you unhappy?" Three-and-a-half-year-old Céline came and put her arms around Zélie.

Zélie smiled. "I am not unhappy; I was just frowning about something I read. Everything is fine."

How can my sister say that I should name my little boy François instead of Joseph? It is as if she thinks that Saint Joseph has taken my other boys from me! If the baby is another boy, he will still be named after Saint Joseph. I like the name. I suppose it's only natural that my sister would like her order's founder, Saint Francis de Sales, to have another namesake. At least she hasn't told me to name a daughter after her order's foundress, Saint Jane Frances de Chantal, or the Visitation Nun Blessed Margaret Mary Alacoque!

The days were shorter and colder now. Léonie was bundled up warmly every day and taken to school by Louise or Louis. At home Zélie and Louis fretted over finding a wet nurse. They had not found one they trusted. This time they were offering room and board at their house, but there was no one suitable. Zélie ardently prayed that their problem might be solved miraculously and that she would be able to nurse her child successfully.

Christmas came, and the older girls arrived home. New Year's Day 1873 came and passed without event. *My New Year's present is coming late!* Zélie thought.

The next day, January 2, was a Thursday. It was Isidore's thirty-second birthday. In the late evening, Zélie did not feel well. At eleven-thirty she gave birth to her "little one."

"A little girl! I was so sure for the last two months that you were a little boy! You are so strong and healthy! Please, God, help our little Thérèse stay healthy." She and Louis had decided that if their child was a girl, they would name her Marie-Françoise-Thérèse: Marie for the Blessed Mother; Françoise—that would please Élise; and Thérèse, in honor of the great Carmelite saint Teresa of Avila. They would call her Thérèse.

The next morning the doorbell rang. Louis answered it. The little boy whose family the Martins had helped stood there.

"My father told me to give this to you and to tell you thank you very much." He extended an envelope to Louis.

Louis smiled and took it. He was pleased to see the boy. "How are your parents?"

"Fine. They said I must not disturb you for long on this happy day. They pray that your wife and child are doing well."

"Thank your parents very much for their prayers. My wife and little Thérèse are fine, but tell your parents to keep praying."

The little boy said he would, then he hurried away toward his home. Louis closed the door and walked upstairs. He would open the note with Zélie.

They opened the note and read the poem inscribed in it.

> Smile and grow up with speed.
> All summon you to joy;
> Gentle care, tender love.
> Yes, smile at the dawn,
> Bud just unclosed,
> You shall be a rose some day!

"Isn't that sweet!" Zélie said.

"Yes, and appropriate," Louis added.

Zélie was looking forward to Thérèse's baptism on Saturday, January 4. Marie, almost thirteen years old, would be the godmother, and Paul-Albert Boul, the young son of friends, would be the godfather. He could not arrive in town until Saturday, so they had to wait for him. Zélie never wanted to wait for baptism. "The sooner she is a child of God, the better!"

January 4 came. Zélie and Louise wrapped little Thérèse in warm blankets. The maid carried Thérèse to Notre-Dame, escorted by Louis and his four daughters. Madame Martin and the Boul family met them at the church. Zélie was staying at home until she was back to her normal strength. Father Lucian Dumaine, another family friend, would baptize Thérèse.

Louis stood there happily as he heard Father Dumaine say, "Marie-Françoise-Thérèse, I baptize you in the name of the Father, and of the Son, and of the Holy Spirit." *She is now a child of God!*

Thérèse seemed to be able to nurse, but Zélie worried that her milk was insufficient and supplemented with a bottle. Then Thérèse did not want to nurse, but wanted only the bottle. Zélie worried, but Thérèse was growing well. Everyone said she was a beautiful baby. When she was happy, she had a darling laugh.

It was not long, though, before Thérèse fell ill. *Oh no! It has happened! I must write to Élise and ask her to pray like she did for Léonie. I am so glad Isidore is coming tonight for a few days. He will have good advice.*

Isidore arrived, and Thérèse recovered.

Then a letter arrived from Le Mans. Sister Marie-Dosithée wrote that she was praying ardently to Saint Francis de Sales and had vowed that if Thérèse were cured, Thérèse would be called by the name Françoise instead of Thérèse. She was certain Zélie would agree with this.

"Well, I don't!" Zélie exclaimed after reading it aloud to Louis. "I like the name Françoise, but not as much as Thérèse. Why should it matter to Saint Francis if I call her Thérèse? Saint Francis, as great a saint as he is, is not in charge of Heaven!"

"No, he isn't. Anyway, Thérèse has recovered!"

"Yes, before Élise's crazy vow was even made."

Thérèse was now two months old, and she was sick again. Zélie called the doctor, who said the baby needed to be breast-fed immediately; nothing else would be enough. Zélie knew she could not do it. How could she get a wet nurse out of thin air? Louis was away on business. *What can I do? . . . Rose! She has a baby! I could go to Semallé!*

"Dr. Belloc, do you think a nursing mother whose child is more than a year older than Thérèse might be able to feed her, or will her milk be too advanced?"

Dr. Belloc was silent for a moment. Then he said adamantly, "If she is your only option to try to save Thérèse, go hire the woman."

Zélie had to wait for morning to start the trip. The first rays of dawn were lighting up the horizon when she left the house by herself. Louise would care for Thérèse and the girls while Zélie was gone. Thérèse had taken only a little milk during the night, and Zélie was very anxious.

Zélie held her shawl tightly around her shoulders. The March air was brisk as she walked along a deserted country road. Birds chirped in the trees, and a nearby rooster crowed a third time. Zélie wished she could walk faster.

Suddenly in front of her, two men stepped out of a bush. Their clothes were unkempt and their hair straggly. There was something about their demeanor that made Zélie nervous, but all she could think of was Thérèse. Rose's home was on the other side of the two men. Zélie said a prayer and continued on her way, looking neither right nor left. The men let her pass and did not follow her. She breathed a sigh of relief.

She passed a beautiful chateau. *Some people think wealth*

will make them happy; it certainly doesn't. True happiness will be when Louis and I are in Heaven with our children. "Thérèse is Yours, God, but please leave her with me."

Zélie finally reached Rose's cottage. Moïes, her husband, was working in the field. Two of their children, twelve-year-old Rose and ten-year-old Auguste, waved from the barnyard, where they were caring for the animals. Zélie knocked on the cottage door.

Rose Taillé opened it. Behind her stood seven-year-old Marie and one-year-old Eugène. "Madame Martin! What a surprise! Come in. Is everything all right?"

"No. My two-month-old Thérèse is dying. I think you might be able to save her. Please come to my house."

"I don't know if I'll be able to save her. Marie, run outside and ask your father to come in." Rose called after her, "Get Rose and Auguste too."

Rose talked with her husband and children. They could manage one week without her. After that she would have to return home with Thérèse.

Rose quickly packed her bag. Half an hour after Zélie's arrival, Rose was ready to go to Alençon. She hugged her children, gave the older ones detailed instructions about caring for their younger siblings, and embraced her husband. Then the two women left.

They had not gone far when Auguste ran up to them out of breath.

"Papa needs you back home. Marie burned herself and is crying, and Eugène is crying also."

"Is Marie burned badly?"

"No. She is just upset."

"Tell Papa I must go help Thérèse. Marie will be fine. Rose is a second mother to Eugène and can make him happy. You will survive without me for one week; Thérèse cannot. If you need help, ask a neighbor."

As Auguste ran off toward home, Rose said to Zélie, "It will probably be good for them this week. They will be much more capable when I return."

~

The maid was sitting in the kitchen holding Thérèse. She looked at the women sadly as they entered. "I have not been able to get her to drink anything."

Rose took Thérèse. She shook her head as if to say, "There is no hope."

Zélie could not stay in the room any longer. She ran upstairs to her room and knelt in front of her statue of Saint Joseph. Tears were streaming down her cheeks. "Please, Saint Joseph, intercede for my little one. Yet not my will but God's be done."

Should I go downstairs? I am not sure I can handle going down, and I might make things worse. At least up here I am praying, Zélie thought. *But no, I can't handle the suspense. It is so quiet downstairs.* She stood up, dried her face, and started for the stairs.

Rose was sitting in a chair holding Thérèse. Thérèse was nursing ravenously. Zélie did not say a word. Two of her lace workers had stopped in to check on them. There was silence in the room.

Thérèse stopped eating. She started coughing violently, and then she fell back against Rose. Everyone was stunned. One of the lace workers started crying. Zélie felt unable to move. *Is she dying? . . . Oh no! She doesn't seem to be breathing!*

Rose put her head against Thérèse's chest. She shook her head. "I can't tell if she is still living."

Zélie put her head against Thérèse to listen. She could hear and feel nothing. For fifteen minutes the women sat there, hoping to see a sign of life. Thérèse looked so calm and peaceful. Zélie, too sad to cry, could only utter a prayer of gratitude. "Since she was going to die, thank You, God, for letting Thérèse die so gently."

Suddenly Thérèse opened her eyes! Her little mouth went into a smile!

"She's cured!" one of the lace workers exclaimed.

Rose put Thérèse in Zélie's arms. Thérèse's color was returning, and she looked cheerful again. The kitchen was filled with rejoicing.

"You're alive, my precious!" Zélie hugged Thérèse. "God, You didn't take her from me!"

Rose remained the week and then left with Thérèse for the Taillé home. It was hard to see them go, but Zélie was hopeful.

~

On Saturday evening, the day before Palm Sunday, the Martins, very faithful in keeping the Lenten fast, had already had their light supper. Louis had settled himself in a chair in the sitting room to read while Céline played with blocks at his feet. He could hear Zélie and Léonie in the kitchen with Louise. He opened his book and started to read.

Ding-dong. Someone was at the front door. Louis arose and opened it. In the shadowy light he saw Vital Romet with Marie. She looked sick and feverish.

"Marie! Vital! What happened?" Louis took Marie's hand and called to his wife. "Zélie, come here!"

"I am not feeling well, Papa," Marie said quietly.

"The sisters asked me to escort her home," Vital explained. "The doctor in Le Mans does not think it is serious, but Sister Marie-Dosithée thought it was better that she be at home."

Zélie appeared.

"Mama, I don't feel well."

"My poor Marie. Come, I will help you get comfortable in bed, and Louise can make you some broth."

Zélie led Marie up the stairs. She was very worried; although the doctor had said it was not serious, Marie looked extremely ill. *What if he was wrong?* After helping her get ready for bed, Zélie brought her a cup of broth.

"It is so hard to swallow," Marie said, slowly sipping from the cup.

"I can tell. You have drunk enough. Why don't you lie down. I'll get some wet cloths to cool your forehead."

During the long night, Marie became delirious. Louis stood watch, worrying. "Go to bed," Zélie told him. "We will have to take turns staying up."

Marie kept muttering, "Take away the ball from my pillow."

"There is no ball on your pillow, dear," Zélie would reply.

Several hours later, Marie's fever went down, and she came to her senses. "I thought my head was a ball. Now it feels like a block of wood." Marie fell asleep, but she looked deathly pale.

Zélie went to get Louis. "I will go to the five-thirty Mass in the morning. On the way home, I will get the doctor. Marie is worse, but the fever has broken. She is sleeping now. You will have to take the little girls to the High Mass without me."

"All right. Get some sleep now, and I will watch over Marie." Louis got out of bed, put on a robe and slippers, and left for Marie's room.

Zélie called on the doctor after Mass. He immediately came to the Martin home. The doctor, showing deep concern, felt Marie's hot forehead and talked with her.

"It is good you came home when you did," he said to his patient.

The doctor motioned to Zélie that he wanted to speak privately with her. They stepped outside the bedroom.

"What is it, Doctor?"

"I fear it is typhoid fever; all of the symptoms indicate it."

"Typhoid? Oh no!" Zélie knew that typhoid fever was often deadly. "What can be done?" she asked the doctor.

"I will write down instructions. You will have to prevent your other children from coming in contact with her. The house will need to be quiet. Typhoid fever should not last longer then twenty-one days. Marie said she first felt sick last Sunday—presumably in two weeks she should start to recover."

"Two whole weeks! My daughter Pauline is supposed to be coming home for Easter vacation. Do you think it is safe for her to come?"

"Only if she can avoid visiting her sister."

That is impossible, Zélie thought. *Marie and Pauline are inseparable. Pauline will have to stay at the convent during the vacation.*

The Martin house became very quiet. Céline was sent every day to the Tessiers' across the street: their daughter, Philomène, entertained her. Léonie, sullen as usual, spent her days with the maid or with friends of the family. Zélie, Louis, and Louise took turns caring for Marie; Marie, however, wanted her mother constantly. Eventually it was necessary to seek outside help

—a Sister of Mercy, from a religious order that cared for the sick in their own homes, was very helpful.

Zélie sent arts and crafts supplies to Pauline to keep her occupied during her break. Marie's fever lingered on day after day. Some days she was better, and then she would have a relapse.

One night Marie kept calling to her mother and saying things that made no sense. Zélie felt overwhelmed and frightened.

"Mama, I took a Host. I am going to the prison. It's for the prisoners. They are going to be very happy."

What does she mean? She must be thinking of Saint Tarsicius, who brought the Holy Eucharist to the Christian prisoners. I want my Marie back, not a Saint Tarsicius!

Louis decided to make a pilgrimage to La Butte Chaumont, a nearby mountain where a holy hermit had lived. He was invoked to cure fevers.

Slowly Marie started to recover. As she recuperated, she began to feel better, but she was bored. Zélie invented games and activities for her to do in bed.

It was an important day when Marie was finally able to go downstairs for a little while. On Ascension Thursday she was well enough to go out to Mass.

The family was looking forward to the following week. Mademoiselle Pauline Romet was going to bring Pauline home. She would arrive Saturday evening. On the next day, Pentecost, Alençon was going to have an exposition. There would be a weeklong celebration with fireworks and balloons in conjunction with it.

Pauline would certainly enjoy her vacation. Louis was going to rent a carriage and take the whole family to see Thérèse.

Rose had been bringing Thérèse to the Martin house when she came to town to sell her butter; however, the Martin family had not been able to travel to Semallé because of Marie's illness. Little Thérèse did not want Rose to leave her sight. When she was at the Martin house she would cry until she was reunited with Rose; then she would laugh and smile. If she was with Rose, she would be content staying at the marketplace all morning. Zélie was looking forward to resuming her day trips to the farm.

When Pauline arrived home she was greeted with hugs and kisses. Everyone wanted to hug her at once. Louis and Zélie marveled at how much taller she had grown.

On Pentecost, after Mass, the Martins spent the day at home for Marie to rest, but with Pauline home everything was a party. Finally, Zélie had to insist that Pauline and the little girls play in the garden while Marie rested.

Monday was a beautiful day. Louis got the carriage early in the morning. The Martins bounced their way along the country roads to Semallé. The countryside in early June was picturesque and charming: wildflowers dotted the roadsides, and birds sang to their hearts' delight.

The Taillé family eagerly welcomed them. Rose had made a lovely dinner to celebrate. Thérèse was quite happy to see them, since Rose was still in her sight. All of her sisters enjoyed holding her. Thérèse especially liked watching Céline play peek-a-boo and make funny faces at her.

"She is becoming a little farm girl," Zélie told Rose. "She is so strong and healthy! Thank you for your great care for her."

"It is a pleasure. She is a delightful baby and very smart."

After the meal, the adults sat outside in the shade of a tree. Thérèse lay content on Zélie's lap. The Taillé children showed the Martin girls the farm. After Marie joined the adults to rest, the other children sought another amusement.

"Pauline," Marie Taillé said, "Thérèse really likes rides. Let's give her one!"

"How?"

"We put hay in the wheelbarrow, and then Thérèse has a nice carriage!"

"And a funny-looking one! Let's see if we can do it."

"I am sure we can. Auguste, put hay in the wheelbarrow. I'll go get Thérèse."

Before long, Thérèse was smiling and laughing as the girls pushed her across the fields in the "carriage." Her ride ended when they reached their parents, who also had a good laugh.

All too soon Louis informed his family that they must leave to arrive home before dark. Sadly the children bid each other good-bye as the Martins climbed into the carriage.

The ride home went quickly. They arrived back in Alençon in time for the fireworks and the torchlight procession that threaded its way through the streets. It was a wonderful ending to an exciting day.

11

PRICKLY PROBLEMS

ZÉLIE SAT WITH HER SISTER-IN-LAW, Céline, on a promenade overlooking the sea. Zélie had taken Marie and Pauline to Lisieux to visit Isidore's family. Today they had traveled to the seashore town of Trouville. The English Channel in front of them glistened in the September sunlight. Along its edge, Marie and Pauline were walking with their uncle, Isidore, and their cousins, Jeanne and Marie. They made a pretty picture with the sparkling water.

"Marie and Pauline are really enjoying the sea," Zélie remarked.

"We are so glad you could come with the older girls, Zélie. After the scare with Marie, it is so good to see her running on the sand."

"Yes, by the time school resumes in October she should be strong enough to return to Le Mans. Pauline missed her greatly. I hope Marie readjusts to school life easily; she is shy and self-conscious. She and lively Pauline are very close even though they are so different. As you know, Léonie is my biggest challenge: at ten years of age she can barely read and write."

"Do you think Sister Marie-Dosithée can help her?"

"That is what I hope, but Léonie must mature more before she can go back there. This autumn she will be having private classes with a young lady who has an advanced diploma. Hopefully she can teach her something. I will be teaching Céline at home for now because her health is so delicate."

"Mama!" Pauline ran up to her mother. "Look at the beautiful shell I just found!"

"It is beautiful." Zélie admired the dainty white shell.

"It is so much fun here at the sea," Pauline said to her aunt. "We are having such a great time!" Then she ran back toward the water and the others.

"You are a good hostess," Zélie said to Céline. "The reception yesterday was magnificent. Now we are at the sea, and tomorrow we will be at your mother's country house visiting your sister's family. Marie and Pauline will talk about this trip for months to come."

"Since you have such a short time, we must use each moment."

"Indeed. Louis and the little girls cannot survive without me for long."

Zélie and Céline joined the others on the sand. Zélie watched a fisherman, standing knee deep in the water, waiting for a catch. *I feel like a fish out of water. I am so lost in this world of parties and pleasures. What gives me the most joy is seeing my girls have fun, and spending time with Isidore and Céline.* Zélie looked at the vast sea spread before her. *I miss Louis and my other children. My world is caring for my family and piecing together lace to provide for my darlings.*

The girls were very sad when the time came to go home, whereas Zélie was interiorly rejoicing that she would soon see Louis and the little girls.

~

On the eve of All Saints' Day, Louis, carrying a small bag, bid his family a good-night. He left the house and waited for Monsieur Tessier to come out of the prefecture. Together they walked to Our Lady of Loreto Chapel, where they participated in a group that held nocturnal Adoration. The Blessed Sacrament would be exposed in a monstrance, and the men would take turns staying up at night praying. Louis always looked forward to nocturnal Adoration.

The men dropped off their personal effects in the room above the sacristy and spent some time greeting others. Then they went to the chapel and knelt as the priest placed the Holy Eucharist in the monstrance. They sang a hymn and recited the opening prayers aloud. *We are given the chance, like Peter, James, and John, to stay awake an hour and keep watch with the Lord*, thought Louis. *I am just like the apostles: very tired. Why am I so exhausted this evening?*

After the opening prayers the men went into the sacristy to decide, by drawing lots, who would take each hour. Afterward Louis would often trade his lot for another's and give that person a more convenient time. Louis liked praying in the wee hours of the morning. When the men were not praying, they would rest in beds in the sacristy's upper room. This evening Louis asked a friend, Monsieur de Morel, to draw for him.

"I need to take a brief rest," Louis told him.

He was climbing the stairs when he smelled smoke coming from the bedroom. "Fire!" Louis yelled.

There were sounds of hurried footsteps behind him. Louis took a deep breath and opened the bedroom door. He looked inside the smoky room.

The stove in the room had been lit earlier. Two beds were touching it and had caught on fire. Louis opened the windows so that the burning mattresses could be thrown outside. Other men appeared with buckets of water and cloths to suffocate the flames. The men worked nonstop until the fire was extinguished. Then they surveyed the damage. The fire had burned part of the sacristy and some of the wooden beds, but it had not touched the chapel.

"It is my fault," Monsieur Tessier said sadly. "I didn't notice the two beds touching the stove when I lit it."

The priest spoke solemnly. "We must thank God ardently for His protection. He takes care of our weaknesses when we have good intentions. Let's say an Our Father and a Hail Mary every hour in thanksgiving tonight."

All the men heartily agreed. Then they headed to the water pump to wash the soot from their hands and faces. As Louis waited for his turn, he marveled how God used his human weakness, exhaustion, to save the chapel. *Our weaknesses can be a blessing!*

~

The beautiful autumn days were over, and the weather turned cold. Advent would soon begin. Rose continued to bring Thérèse to the Martin house every time she came to town. Thérèse, having grown big and strong, could now stand by holding on to a chair.

Zélie had noticed something peculiar about her youngest child. Thérèse did not like being held by Louise in her maid's outfit, nor did she like her mother's clothes. However, she seemed to be very content when held by the lace workers, who were country women wearing rural dresses.

One Thursday, when Thérèse was visiting, Zélie let the delighted lace workers hold the little girl. She, as usual, was happy in their arms. The doorbell rang. The Martins' friend Madame Tifenne, elegantly attired as usual, stood there. Zélie invited her into the crowded room.

Zélie looked at happy Thérèse and at her fashionably dressed guest. "Would you like to hold my baby?" Zélie asked Madame Tifenne.

"Certainly."

As Madame Tifenne held out her arms for Thérèse, the baby took one look at her and started to cry. She hid her face on the lace worker's sleeve. She peeked out to see if Madame Tifenne was watching her. She was, so Thérèse resumed crying.

"I have never seen the like of her," one of the workers said.

Madame Tifenne stopped looking at Thérèse. Suddenly the baby was happy again. All of the women laughed over Thérèse's aversion to fashionable clothing.

~

The older girls came home for their winter break. In the new year a very excited Léonie returned with her sisters to the convent school. The house seemed almost empty with only Céline at home, but early in April, fifteen-month-old Thérèse came home to stay. She quickly grew accustomed to her new life with her mama and papa, and entertaining big sister Céline.

Meanwhile, the convent school sent bad news: they were having great difficulty with Léonie. Despite her good intentions, she was very undisciplined. One moment she would apologize and promise to be good; the next she would be disobedient again. She was also having trouble learning. She needed a full-time teacher, and the convent did not have the capacity to fulfill her needs. Zélie was very sad when she read her sister's letter.

"God has a plan for Léonie," Louis said, trying to comfort Zélie.

"He does. He miraculously cured her when she was a baby. I was so sure my sister and the other good and patient sisters could work wonders for her."

Léonie came home, and Zélie found new teachers for her. Two religious sisters had moved to Alençon and were fundraising to start an orphanage. So far they had only one child, a little girl from their previous town, but they said they would be happy to teach Léonie.

Little Thérèse was growing well and was very affectionate. Zélie delighted in designing beautiful dresses for her. Céline was also getting stronger and healthier. Louis installed a swing in the backyard for the little girls, which they both enjoyed. Thérèse liked to swing high and had to be tied on with a rope to keep her safe. Zélie was always relieved when Thérèse got off the swing.

~

Summer arrived, and the Guérin family came to spend several days in Alençon. Tourists also came and visited the Martin house to see Alençon lace. They would take up Zélie's time and often not buy any lace.

One day a group of English visitors came to the Martins' door. Zélie showed them her lace and how she made it. The language barrier made communication difficult, but Zélie understood that they wanted to buy one and a half meters of lace.

Zélie tried to talk as clearly as possible. "Lace is one hundred fifty francs per meter."

They nodded to show they understood. Zélie got her scissors and was just about to cut the lace when they handed her the money: seven and a half francs.

Zélie looked bewildered. "No, that is not the price."

"Five francs per meter, right?"

"No! One hundred fifty francs per meter."

The visitors left without buying any. And Zélie thanked God that she had not cut the lace before receiving the money.

~

All too soon October came, and Marie and Pauline returned to school. Thérèse was talking constantly now, but it was hard to understand her. Céline, a smart girl, was being taught at home by Zélie, and Léonie returned to taking classes with the two religious sisters.

Zélie was not pleased with Léonie's schooling. The sisters were not good teachers, and although they treated Léonie well, their eight-year-old charge, Armandine, was overworked and treated poorly.

Zélie told Louis her concern. "I think those women are mistreating Armandine, and I feel I have a duty to report it. She does not look healthy and acts languid, but maybe she is naturally that way."

"Maybe, but what evidence do you have?"

"Léonie's words, and what Louise and I have seen when we escort Léonie to school and back. Armandine is always doing menial tasks and has no time for learning or playing. Also, she is not being fed well. I think we should leave Léonie there—even though she is not receiving the best education—until I am certain that I will not be accusing falsely."

"Very well. Make sure Léonie is fine with the plan, and pack some food for Armandine. Aren't people all over town donating to the sisters' charity?"

"Yes. If I say anything against them, no one will believe me."

Zélie mentioned the problem to her confessor and to her sister. They both said she should take action.

However, she could not come up with a good plan. *People think of the sisters as holy women, and I have no real evidence*.

One day Léonie forgot to bring Armandine's snack. Louise arrived late in the afternoon to escort Léonie home. The maid looked at Armandine. "Are you sick?"

"I have a tummy ache. I'm hungry."

"I forgot to bring the food today. I'm sorry," Léonie said sadly.

"It is not your fault that she is not getting sufficient food," Zélie said later to Léonie.

Then turning to the maid, she told her to serve the meal without her that evening. "I am going to write the priest in Banner. The religious sisters and the little girl are both from there. He should know something about them and be able to contact Armandine's mother. She is a widow who entrusted her child to the sisters since she thought it would be the best for her daughter. I will ask the priest to tell the widow to collect Armandine and place her in the Refuge if she feels she cannot raise her. That school has an excellent reputation for helping homeless children."

The next day Léonie was accompanied by Louise to the sisters' house. Zélie had given her daughter a basket of food and instructed her: "Give this basket to Armandine. Armandine left this basket here the day she came to visit. It is natural that you would be returning it. I have placed bread and jam inside for her. Tell Armandine not to act suspicious with it."

Armandine opened the door. Léonie handed her the basket. "It is for you. Don't hide it beneath your apron. Just carry it. It is your basket."

After Louise left, Armandine looked scared and put the basket under her apron.

"Don't," Léonie whispered.

"I must. They won't allow me to keep it if they see it."

"They won't realize anything is in your basket; they will think I am just returning it."

Refusing to listen to Léonie, Armandine hid the basket under her apron. It created a funny bulge.

"What do you have underneath your apron?" the older woman, Sister Saint-Louis, demanded as Armandine tiptoed past her.

Armandine hesitantly pulled out the basket. Sister Saint-Louis looked inside it. "Bread and jam! Why are you hiding Madame Martin's gift to us?"

An hour later, Zélie was piecing lace together. The little girls were playing upstairs, Louise was working in the kitchen, and Louis was away on business. Zélie was enjoying the quiet until the doorbell rang. She got up to answer it.

Sister Saint-Louis was standing there.

"Come in." Zélie was anxious. *The Lord has arranged this; it is time I tell her what I think.*

Sister Saint-Louis entered and abruptly asked her question: "Why did you give Armandine food?"

"Sister Saint-Louis, I sent the food because the little

girl is not getting enough to eat. There are many kind people in town giving food, clothing, and money to help you start your orphanage. Why doesn't Armandine get to eat the food or wear the dresses donated to you?"

Sister Saint-Louis laughed as Zélie spoke. "You really don't understand Armandine. She gets enough to eat. She has to work hard, but all of us do. Armandine can be a very selfish girl. We must not spoil her. We have to make her a saint."

"But not a martyr! If I give her food, you must promise to let her eat it."

Sister Saint-Louis took Zélie's hand. "I cannot promise that. The food might not be good for her."

Sister Saint-Louis left the house, laughing. As the door closed behind the sister, Zélie sank into a chair. She was very disturbed and puzzled by Sister Saint-Louis, who seemed to laugh at everything.

That evening Louise went to get Léonie. When they arrived home, Louise said Sister Saint-Louis had been crying and saying Zélie was persecuting her, that this would be just another pearl in her heavenly crown.

What a hypocrite, Zélie thought. She could not wait to discontinue Léonie's lessons, but if she did not send Léonie back the next day, Saturday, the sisters would not allow Armandine to visit the Martins on Sunday.

The next day Zélie went to the Refuge. The superior said that they did not have room, but because of the seriousness of the case, they would make a place for the little girl. *These are sisters I admire,* Zélie thought as she walked home. *Their works bear good fruit.*

Armandine visited the Martins on Sunday. She acted as if she was sore, and her face was pale. Zélie had a good, kind talk with her.

Armandine said, "They beat me, but since you talked with them they have been nice and giving me lots of food. They say all sorts of dreadful things about you, Madame Martin."

"There is a nice school called the Refuge for children who need homes. The students are treated very well there. I have asked the priest in Banner to tell your mother to come place you in the school. I am sure she wants to do what is best for you. Hopefully she will arrive in town soon."

"Thank you!" Armandine said excitedly.

That night Zélie wrote a letter to the sisters. She made sure it was grammatically correct and beautifully written. In it she explained that Léonie would be suspending lessons with them and why.

On Tuesday a woman appeared at the Martin house. Zélie hoped it was Armandine's mother. The woman asked to speak to Zélie.

"I am she."

"I prepare lace for Armandine to make. I was just at the sisters' home, and Armandine asked me to find you. She wants her mama to come now since the sisters are making her so unhappy."

Zélie sighed. "I can't make her mama magically appear, and I can't legally take her from the sisters.

Tomorrow I will send Louise and Léonie to the house. I have to pay the sisters for the last few lessons."

The next day a visitor came to the Martins' door. It was Sister Saint-Louis. She was pretending to cry. *What an actress she is*, Zélie thought. Sister Saint-Louis recollected herself and spoke sweetly to exonerate herself.

After listening to Sister Saint-Louis' ramblings for a quarter of an hour, Zélie interrupted. "You use the language of a saint; in fact, the saints spoke no better than you"—Sister Saint-Louis' face glowed with the compliment—"but do you regret what you have made the child endure?"

Sister Saint-Louis' mask of gentleness disappeared. Her face became fierce and harsh. "Everything you have said is a lie! We have never treated the child badly."

Zélie was fuming inside, but she managed to hold back her anger. "You mistreat the child, starve her, beat her, and make her your slave."

Sister Saint-Louis was having trouble keeping herself composed. She left in a rush. *What will happen next?* Zélie thought.

Later that day, a letter arrived from the priest in Banner. Zélie quickly opened it.

"Thank you very much for your letter. I know the two women of whom you wrote: they are not religious sisters. They are masquerading as religious for their own benefit. I threw them out of my parish. I will inform the child's mother as quickly as possible. She lives a distance from here."

Zélie was stunned to hear the truth about the two women. *I hope Armandine's mother comes very soon before anything more happens. I am so worried for that child's safety!*

The next day a woman whom Zélie knew stopped by to visit. It was obvious that the fraudulent sisters had sent her. Zélie knew her as a good woman, but gullible. The visitor knew a lot of Zélie's plans for Armandine, which only the little girl had been told. Zélie worriedly wondered how much Sister Saint-Louis knew.

On Saturday afternoon, Zélie noticed a woman stop at their partially opened window. "Excuse me," the woman called. She seemed distraught. Zélie went to the window.

"Is house number thirty-six nearby?" the woman asked.

"Yes, this is it. You must be Armandine's mother!"

"Yes, I am! I finally found you, Madame. Please help me. Something terrible has happened!"

Zélie rushed to open the door. Louis, home from his trip, heard the commotion and ran to the front room.

Armandine's mother spoke with anguish. "I went to the sisters' house to get Armandine. We were just ready to leave. In fact, we were standing in the doorway when the sisters opened a window and started to yell, 'Help! Kidnapper! Help! Child abductor!' A crowd quickly gathered, and four strong men tore Armandine from me. Meanwhile, the sisters were spewing foolish words against you, Madame, and at me.

"I finally escaped from them. Then I realized that the letter with your address was missing; it must have fallen out of my pocket during the scuffle. I could remember only your street number and not your street name. I have gone from street to street looking for you. I would have gone directly to the police, but I feared they wouldn't believe me."

Zélie was horrified. "What do we do?"

"We will go to the police station," Louis said.

Louis and Zélie put on their coats, and the three headed out. Zélie approached the police station holding Louis' hand. Even though her father had been a policeman, she had never been inside a police station. Louis asked for the police chief.

"He is on vacation," the man at the desk said.

The Martins explained the predicament.

"These things always take a while to settle. The police chief might be in tomorrow." The policeman seemed in no hurry to take care of the matter.

Armandine's mother was crestfallen. "I own a small store on a country road. I cannot be gone for long. I was so sure my Armandine was happy. I had just received a letter from her saying she was the happiest girl in Alençon."

"If she was the happiest girl in town, the other children must be like Blessed Benedict Joseph Labre, eating cabbage cores from the garbage!" Louis exclaimed.

"What do we do now?" Armandine's mother asked.

"Pray. God will help us," Zélie responded.

That night Zélie had insomnia. When she finally fell asleep, she dreamed of Armandine, emaciated, begging for help. Sister Saint-Louis appeared in the dream as a diabolical figure. Zélie awoke abruptly. She got up and prayed. "Dear Blessed Mother, under your special title of Our Lady of Perpetual Help, help us." Suddenly an idea came to Zélie. She crept downstairs to her desk, lit a lamp, and started to write a letter. The police commissioner had the power to investigate things!

Louis and Armandine's mother attended the early Mass on Sunday morning while Zélie finished her letter. She was going to make sure the police commissioner understood the urgency of the case. Then Zélie, Louise, and the girls went to the High Mass while Louis and Armandine's mother delivered the letter to the commissioner. Zélie could not concentrate during Mass.

Louis was already home when his family returned from Mass. As he opened the door for them, Zélie sent the girls upstairs with Louise. Then Louis and Zélie went into the sitting room.

"Louis, what happened?"

"The commissioner talked with Armandine's mother after reading the letter. He sent a policeman to get the sisters. The women slandered you. They had tried to go to the public prosecutor's house but had no success. After listening to the women, the commissioner decided that the sisters, Armandine's mother, and you need to go to the courthouse today at one o'clock. Court will be in session because two prisoners escaped last night."

"Must I go to court?" Zélie shivered. *What will happen?*

"Don't worry, God will be with us. Come, you better have something to eat."

"How can I eat? I'm too nervous."

"Zélie, remember that you are the one who rises to difficulties while I fall apart."

"Yes, but you manage daily life better. What will happen?"

Louis and Zélie arrived at the public prosecutor's office only to be told to go to the police station. A very distinguished-looking gentleman approached them at the station. *He must be the public prosecutor*, Zélie thought.

The prosecutor said he had come out of pure kindness; he had very little time, as he was needed in court that day. He said that since the mother was a widow, and had given her child voluntarily to the sisters, she could not take the child back on a whim. The Board of Guardians would have to decide if Armandine's mother was in a position to take back her child. The case did not have the evidence it needed to be decided.

"We have a letter from the priest in Banner, where the sisters are from, stating that the sisters are frauds," Louis told the man.

"That is not enough evidence."

They were led into a room where several important-looking men were present. Zélie saw the sisters sitting there with Armandine. The little girl had a haughty expression on her face that Zélie had never seen before.

Zélie heard one of the officials say, "That child doesn't look starved." *They will be calling me a liar soon. The sisters have convinced everyone.*

Every second seemed like an eternity to Zélie. The sisters were very vocal. Armandine was taken aside to be questioned. When she returned she did not look at Zélie or her mother. *She is betraying us!*

Then Zélie was summoned by the prosecutor to follow him. Zélie stood up hesitantly. *Where is he taking me? Am I going to be arrested? If Armandine has turned against us, I do not have enough evidence to support my case.*

The prosecutor led her to a small room. He pulled out a chair and motioned for her to sit. Then he sat across from her.

"Madame, I need your side of the story."

His kind look gave Zélie the strength she needed. She told the whole story of Armandine's situation. The man listened intently and took notes. Finally Zélie asked, "What did Armandine tell you?"

"She said she felt very well."

"Could you ask her to come in here? She and I could talk in front of you."

"Yes, that is a good idea."

When Armandine appeared, she ignored Zélie. The prosecutor asked her again how she was.

"I am fine. I don't want to go with my mother."

Zélie looked at the prosecutor and then turned to

the girl. "Armandine, for how long have you been fine?"

The child finally allowed her gaze to meet Zélie's. "Madame, since you said everything to the sisters."

"How did they treat you before?"

"They refused to feed me, and they beat me. They made me do everything for them, from buckling their shoes to scrubbing the kitchen floor."

The prosecutor looked intently at Armandine. "Did the sisters give you anything different to eat or drink before coming here?"

"Yes. A strange-tasting drink—I never had it before."

"Alcohol," the prosecutor said softly. "That explains a lot." He turned to Zélie. "I see you are correct. I must talk with the Board of Guardians since the mother has no certificate and you did not know her prior. You may return to the other room. I will have to see if the public prosecutor's office is still meeting. I want to get this settled quickly."

But isn't he the public prosecutor? Zélie was confused.

She returned to the main room and smiled at Louis. Everything was going to work out all right! She was puzzled by the man who had been helping them; clearly he was not the public prosecutor after all. The sisters, seeing Zélie confident, stood up infuriated and started to leave the room. Three policemen stopped them and insisted they sit. Then Sister Saint-Louis quit acting demurely and started to yell what she really thought of everyone. *If the policemen were not holding Sister Saint-Louis back, she would probably attack me.*

Within fifteen minutes the dignified man returned. He looked at the irate, fraudulent sisters; at Armandine's mother; and at the Martins. He spoke solemnly. "Having talked with the governing authorities, we have settled the matter. We are returning the child to the appropriate person." Then he looked at Zélie. "I want to thank you for caring about someone else's child, and I want to commend you for bearing hardship and risking your reputation to let the truth be known." He turned to Louis. "Thank you for supporting your wife through this ordeal."

Sister Saint-Louis and her companion interrupted. "Stop ridiculing us!"

The man turned toward them. "I am not ridiculing you, only praising them. Madame," he said, looking again at Zélie, "I return this child to her mother, but she is also to be under your protection in case there is a change in her situation. Since you wanted very much to take care of her, I am happy to have also been able to help her. It is so beautiful to do good."

The rest of the event went by in a blur to Zélie. Armandine would go home with her mother, who had remarried since giving Armandine to the sisters. If things did not go well, her mother would send her back to Zélie, who would place her at the Refuge. The mother asked the sisters for Armandine's clothes and an umbrella she had lost when she had gone to pick up

Armandine the previous day. Sister Saint-Louis refused the request, and the kind man had to intervene. When everything was settled, Zélie and Louis left.

As they walked out of the police station, the January sun, starting to set, gave the world a golden hue. Louis and Zélie were silent as they headed home, hand in hand.

"Louis, it ended perfectly!"

"Yes, it did. I am proud of you."

"I was so scared. I thought the man we first met was the public prosecutor. If I had realized he was the police commissioner—as he told us at the end—I would not have been so scared. I really thought he was going to sentence me to prison for slander."

"Poor Zélie, I had no clue you thought that. I had met him earlier today when I delivered your letter."

"What a relief it is over. I will be glad to get home and resume daily life."

12

LOURDES

HAVING JUST FINISHED WRITING to her sister-in-law, Zélie sat at her desk perusing the letter. *I certainly wander from thought to thought in it, but it describes my hectic life so well. I have so many trials that if only I did everything for God, I would become a canonized saint!*

"Mama," three-year-old Thérèse interrupted, "I want to give you a hug."

Zélie smiled. *Thérèse is so affectionate that I don't get my work done. What a funny problem to have.*

On a beautiful Sunday in May, the Martin family walked to the countryside after Mass. The wayside meadows and paths were covered with wildflowers, and the girls picked large bouquets to adorn the Blessed Mother statue at home. Louis and Zélie walked in front of the girls. Léonie had refused to accompany them on the walk. New arrangements for her studies had been made, but she was still having trouble.

"Girls," Louis called, "it is time to go home!"

Sixteen-year-old Marie, who had recently graduated, helped her youngest sister with her bouquet. Thérèse's little hands could not carry all the flowers she had picked. She would drop a flower and bend to pick it up; then she would drop two more flowers.

The Martins had reached the outskirts of town when Zélie noticed an elderly, poor man sitting on a tree stump near an abandoned shed. His gray beard was unkempt, but he had a kindly face and smiled at the happy children. Zélie took Thérèse's hand and placed some coins inside it. "Thérèse, give these alms to the man."

Thérèse ran to the man and handed him the gift. He looked at the little girl and smiled gratefully. Then he followed Thérèse to her parents and profusely said his thanks.

Zélie looked at the man. His clothes were ragged and his bare feet bruised. He was very thin and looked starved. "Come to our house. We have an old pair of shoes that I think will fit you, and you must stay for dinner."

"Really?" The man's eyes glistened.

He walked with them to Alençon. After welcoming the man into their home, Zélie handed him Louis' old pair of shoes. His face beamed with joy. Then he partook of dinner as if he had not eaten in a week. Every once in a while he would stop eating to admire his shoes. Afterward he insisted on reciting a prayer that he liked to say at Mass.

"Come again when you need help, and don't hesitate," Zélie told him as he prepared to leave. After his departure Zélie looked at Louis. "Do you think you could get him admittance to the hospice? He would like it, and he needs a better place to live than his abandoned shed."

"I was thinking of the hospice also. I will write the monastery in the morning."

"Mama," little Thérèse cried, running into the room. "Come! I broke your vase."

Zélie followed her to the sitting room. On the floor in pieces was a tiny vase. Zélie stooped to pick up the sharp porcelain and heaved a sigh. She had really liked that vase.

"Mama, Mama, I am so sorry." Thérèse was crying so much that she could barely talk.

"Thérèse, it is all right; I forgive you." Zélie sat down and placed Thérèse on her lap.

Bit by bit, Thérèse stopped crying. "Don't be unhappy, my Little Mama. When I earn a lot of money, I will buy you a new vase. I promise."

Zélie kissed her little girl. "I will look forward to that day. Now put on a smile and go play."

Thérèse disappeared up the stairs. *I wonder what she will become when she is older*, Zélie mused. *She is very intelligent but scatterbrained. Fortunately, she has a heart of gold.*

She recalled Thérèse's conversation from another day.

"Mama, I wish you would die."

"Why?" Zélie scolded her. "You don't say such things to people."

"But I want you to be happy, and you say we have to die to go to Heaven, where we will be always happy," Thérèse had responded.

Zélie had only been able to smile.

~

Louis was walking home from the bank one day. Managing the financial and commercial ends of Zélie's company took a lot of time and effort. It always seemed they had too much or not enough work. Louis was occupied thinking about bills when Zélie met him at the door.

"Louis, please go talk with Marie. She is in the garden crying."

"Why?"

"She doesn't like her new dress. The dress is beautiful and stylish. She thinks it looks like we are trying to marry her off with no delay, even though it is quite modest."

"Where did she get that crazy idea?"

"I think from something Louise said. I have tried talking reason with Marie, but she is still crying. You will probably be better at it. One minute she is complaining that she has a dull life, and the next minute she doesn't want to go to a concert or a party. With clothing she thinks I am never elegant enough, and she wants her little sisters to look as fashionable as the mayor's daughter. Yet she wants to wear plain, old dresses. She is so self-conscious and shy."

Louis found Marie sitting on a bench underneath one of the fruit trees. Her face was red from crying, and she was clutching a handkerchief. She was wearing her beautiful new dress.

"Marie, what is the matter?" he asked.

"Papa, you don't want me to get married quickly like other girls' fathers do, do you?"

"Of course not. Your mother and I do not care if you ever get married." Louis sat down on the bench. "We work hard to make sure our children need not be confined by money, like your mother was. Our only desire for you—as it is for all our children—is that you become the person God created you to be. And that is a saint."

"Yes, Papa."

"The most important thing in life is to do God's will with love; then you will find Life." Louis handed Marie his handkerchief.

"Thanks, Papa." She started to dry her face. "If I don't want to get married or join the religious life, you won't be displeased?"

"No. God calls people to be single also. There are many paths to Him but one God. Think of Blessed Benedict Joseph Labre, the beggar who was recently beatified. He is a wonderful example."

Marie smiled with relief and sat quietly for a few seconds, sniffling. Then she gave her father a hug. "Thank you." She stood up and went back into the house.

Marie found Zélie in the kitchen. "Mama, I am very sorry about earlier."

"Don't worry. None of us is perfect, and second chances are wonderful things."

"I will try to think less of what other people think of me and more about what God desires of me."

"That's my good girl. Don't be a slave to fashion or society; live for God and you will be free. Incidentally, God likes you to look beautiful."

"Then I guess I can like my dress."

Zélie smiled. *That's one problem taken care of, but there will always be another.*

~

Léonie was a perplexing child. She had good intentions, but she was often disobedient, defiant, and aloof. Zélie invented a game to help Léonie conquer her poor behavior. Léonie would place a cork in a certain drawer every time she was good during the day. By evening she would hopefully have a surprise for her mother—a drawer full of corks. Unfortunately, she would frequently forget the game and return to her former ways.

Céline, meanwhile, was often sick. Once Louis and Zélie discovered that she was allergic to cider, life got easier. Being good was natural for her, and she would make countless little sacrifices while playing with Thérèse. Marie had brought back from the convent little strings of beads. Céline would move a bead on the strings every time she did a good deed; she called this discipline her "practices." Playing with Thérèse gave her many opportunities to practice doing good!

Marie had taken over teaching Céline, and three-year-old Thérèse dearly wanted to participate in the lessons. Looking sad, she would lie outside the closed door to the school room. Then the girls would trip over her when they came out. Zélie was informed about Thérèse's behavior and told her she must not do that. Thérèse did it again the next day.

Marie came out of the room and almost fell over her little sister. "Thérèse, why are you doing this again? Jesus is very hurt when Thérèse is naughty."

Thérèse listened very intently; she did not want Jesus

to be hurt. She never lay down in front of the door again.

Louis loved to take the girls to the Pavilion. During the springtime they would pick delicious produce from Louis' garden or they would play a game on the grass.

It was with sadness that Zélie learned that her sister's tuberculosis had returned. On top of that, Zélie was having her own health problems. She had had a funny, small lump on her breast for many years, and now it was starting to hurt. Zélie decided she would mention it to Isidore when he and his family came for summer vacation. Being a pharmacist, he was good at offering remedies and practical advice.

Isidore did not like the look of Zélie's little "booboo," as she called it. He suggested some treatments. "If it shows no sign of improvement, you had better see a doctor."

Zélie decided to try his treatments and continue her daily life as normal, offering her suffering to God. *By giving God my suffering, I become more united to Jesus on the cross. Jesus will use my suffering to bring me and others to Himself.*

When the treatments brought no improvement, Zélie went to a doctor.

After examining her, the doctor looked grave. "You have a very serious tumor. All I can offer you is an operation. Would you be too afraid to have one?"

"No," Zélie paused, "but is the operation often successful?"

"The results are very uncertain."

"Is there one chance in a hundred that the operation would cure me?"

The doctor looked intently at Zélie for a moment. "I would not necessarily advise an operation in your situation."

"Thank you for being frank." Zélie felt a pang of concern as she thought of her family. "How long do women live with this condition?"

"It depends. Some for many years." The doctor reached for a pen. "I can write you a prescription; would you like one?"

"What would the medicine do?"

The doctor hesitated and then spoke candidly. "It only helps patients feel better."

"Then no, thank you."

When Zélie got home she told the family: "I have breast cancer." The girls started to cry. As she tried to comfort them, she regretted her sudden announcement.

Louis, who had wanted Zélie to see a doctor, took the news extremely hard. He lost all interest in his fishing and going to the Vital Romet Club. In fact, he put his lines away in the attic. He was very worried about Zélie.

Isidore and Céline were also grief stricken. Upon

everyone's advice, Zélie went to Lisieux to see a noted surgeon. Doctor Notta's diagnosis was that it was far too late to operate.

"Nothing can be done," he said.

Something can be done, Zélie thought. *Pray! If God wants me to die from this, then I will try to be ready. At least I have time to prepare. Or God could easily perform a miracle for the sake of the children. If this keeps getting worse, I will go to Lourdes. So many miracles have happened there. If Louis had had his way, I would have already gone!*

Despite her cancer, Zélie was enjoying family life. Céline and Thérèse continued to entertain their family. Rose Taillé had given Thérèse a bantam rooster and hen. Thérèse, in turn, gave the rooster to Céline. Every evening, Céline would catch the rooster and hen out in the yard and bring them inside to play with them. The little girls would occupy themselves that way until they had to go to bed. Zélie enjoyed watching them.

One evening at bedtime, Thérèse, hugging Céline, declared, "We are like the little white hens; we can't be separated."

Marie started giving Thérèse lessons and allowing her to attend Céline's classes. She was a good student, willing to sit quietly and learning quickly.

Pauline came home for winter break, and Thérèse turned four. Zélie told Pauline about her ailment; she had not written Pauline about it beforehand because she did not want to distract her from her studies. Zélie made light of her illness, because they had another sorrow in their lives: Sister Marie-Dosithée was dying from tuberculosis. The Visitation Sisters suggested that Pauline not return to school after the break, since it would be hard on her, but Pauline insisted on going back, saying, "I would like to be near my aunt."

One Saturday evening Louis went to a formal dinner at Vital Romet's house. At home Louise was preparing the dinner and drying dishes. The January sun set early, and the light in the room was dim. The aroma of purée of pea soup drifted through the air.

"Léonie," she ordered, "come help."

The girl hurried in and obediently started to help her.

"Louise," Thérèse requested, walking into the room, "please help me get my little fisherman from the shelf. I can't reach it."

"All right." Louise smiled at darling Thérèse. "Léonie, the soup is ready. Slice the bread, put it in the soup tureen, and ladle the soup over it. Don't spill it!" She left the room with Thérèse.

Léonie did as she was told. She carefully cut the bread and dropped it into the tureen. She managed to spoon the soup into the dish without spilling a drop. *It certainly smells good.*

Shortly thereafter the family sat down at the dinner table. They all bowed their heads and made the sign of the cross. Zélie recited a prayer and then removed the cover from the soup tureen.

"Purée of pea soup, my favorite!" Marie exclaimed.

"Poor Papa at Monsieur Vital's grand dinner. He will have nothing as good as this!"

Zélie picked up a soup bowl and reached for the ladle, which was floating on top of the soup. *How strange*, she thought. She tried to push the ladle deeper; it would not fill with soup. Zélie peered at the soup. In the candlelight it looked normal. She tried to stir the soup; it was extremely thick. "Louise, what did you put in here?"

"Madame, I made it just like normal."

Zélie continued trying to stir the soup. She decided there must be a foreign object in it. Every time she tried to get the mysterious thing on the spoon, it would slide back into the purée. Louise was very puzzled, and the girls started to laugh.

Finally Zélie got the thing on the spoon. She pulled it high into the air. It was a very thick object and looked hardly suitable for eating. Everyone was quiet as she let the soup drip off it into the tureen.

"It's my dishtowel!" Louise exclaimed. "How did it get in there?"

"I never looked inside before putting in the bread," Léonie said, crestfallen. "I'm sorry."

Marie looked sadly at her empty bowl; the little girls laughed; and behind Zélie's back, Louise glared at Léonie.

Zélie smiled. "There is no harm done. We have other food to eat. Laughter is a good thing."

~

Sister Marie-Dosithée's illness was advanced and even though she was not expected to recover, she was at peace. "If God is calling me home, I am eager to go to Him." In fact, Sister Marie-Dosithée was displeased that the community was making a novena to Father Claude de la Colombière, confessor to Blessed Margaret Mary Alacoque. If Sister Marie-Dosithée were healed, the cure could be used for Father de la Colombière's beatification. Zélie thought that if her sister was not eager for a miracle, then maybe the prayers should be for her, Zélie. She certainly did not feel in a hurry to leave this earth, and she was not prepared like her sister. Everyone thought of Sister Marie-Dosithée as a living saint.

A miracle did not happen; on February 24, 1877, Sister Marie-Dosithée died. One of her fellow religious sisters wrote Zélie later that day. The letter said that Sister Marie-Dosithée had died a holy and peaceful death. Shortly beforehand she had been blessing the Martin and Guérin families. "We all have a special protector interceding for us now," the sister wrote, "for it would be hard to live a more virtuous life and die a more saintly death."

Zélie read the letter over and over. It also said that Pauline took the news hard but that her faith gave her courage. *I wish I could have been there too in her last weeks. She always cared so much about me, even from afar. She meant a lot to my three older daughters. Marie would listen to her when she would not listen to anyone else. Pauline has been very inspired by Élise. I suspect Pauline will follow in her aunt's footsteps and enter the religious life. A part of me will find that sacrifice very hard. And Léonie wants to be just like her aunt. It is perplexing how a child who is often defiant and interested only in earthly things is then writing a letter to her aunt with requests for Heaven.*

Zélie recalled Léonie's letter; she had asked her aunt to pray that she might be "a true religious." When Marie had wanted her to erase the word *true*, Léonie had responded, "I want to keep it that way. It means I want to be a completely good religious and in the end a saint!" Zélie had been startled by Léonie's words. On earth Élise had not been able to help Léonie, but maybe she would be able to succeed now. *I will beg her intercession for Léonie.*

~

It was two weeks later when Marie came into the sitting room with an odd expression on her face. "Mama, I need to talk with you privately."

"All right, let's go sit in my bedroom."

"What is it?" Zélie asked once they were seated.

"I think I know what is plaguing Léonie. Louise has traumatized her into blind obedience."

"What! Louise can be insensitive and demanding—I have had to tell her not to scold the children for their little faults—but how can she be traumatizing Léonie? In fact, Léonie seems to want to be only with her!"

"I know, that's just it; Louise scolds Léonie for not helping her."

"Really? I was so sure the girls liked being with Louise."

"Céline and Thérèse do. Louise spoils them. I just went into the kitchen, and I saw Louise hit Léonie."

"What?" Zélie rose to her feet quickly. "Where are they?"

"Léonie is in the laundry room now, and Louise is in the kitchen. Wait! Let me tell you the rest of it since they are both in separate rooms."

"Yes."

"I heard Louise scolding Léonie. I went into the kitchen to see what was the problem. They didn't realize I was there. Léonie was crying. Louise said Léonie deserved to have her ears boxed for being tardy."

"Oh no!"

"Louise slapped Léonie on the cheek. Then Léonie ran to the laundry room crying. I left without Louise seeing me. At one point during the scene, Louise said, 'Since your parents do not know how to control an unruly child, I must.'"

"How could she think or say that? And it is none of her business! She is not a parent. Poor Léonie! I must go find her. Then I will deal with the maid."

Zélie went downstairs to the laundry room. Léonie stood there folding napkins. Her face was red from crying and the slap, but her demeanor showed her customary defiance.

"Yes, Mama?"

"Léonie—" Zélie hesitated; there was so much to

say. "Léonie, I am so sorry that Louise hit you, and I am extremely displeased with her."

Léonie looked very awkward and uncomfortable.

"Léonie, let's sit on this bench and have a little talk. I want to know why Louise has been treating you harshly."

Léonie sat down next to her mother. She started to cry.

Zélie handed her a handkerchief and put an arm around her. "It's all right to cry. I'll wait until you're ready to talk."

An hour later Marie came into the laundry room. Léonie was clasped in their mother's arms. Zélie had tears in her eyes, but Léonie was beaming.

It was very hard for Zélie to talk with the maid; for Louise, however, it was even harder. Her kind employer was very displeased with her.

"How could you treat anyone like you treated Léonie? You abused and harshly scolded her. No wonder she preferred our displeasure to your punishments."

"Please, I was only trying to help. You know Léonie is an insubordinate child."

"I know, but brutality never converted anyone; it just turns people into slaves."

"Please don't fire me."

"I won't. I ask you to leave as soon as you can acquire another job. Léonie is scared of you. You are not to direct even one word toward her."

"Yes, Madame."

Now that the maid had no control over Léonie, the child rapidly changed. She became affectionate and playful. Zélie and Louis were delighted and thankful. With a lot of gentle, loving care they were sure that Léonie would be able to overcome her difficult nature.

If only I am cured so that I can finish raising her, Zélie frequently thought.

Zélie had decided it was time to take a pilgrimage to Lourdes. Many people had been cured at the miraculous spring the Blessed Mother had revealed to Bernadette Soubirous in 1858, just nineteen years prior. Louis offered to go with her and plan a nice relaxing trip, but Zélie declined.

"I want to make a pilgrimage and not add on a pleasure trip. You know I prefer to be at home rather than traveling. I think Léonie should go with me; it would be good for her. I would also like to take Marie and Pauline. They would be able to help me and Léonie."

After much discussion and planning, Louis made arrangements for Zélie and the three older girls to accompany some pilgrims from a nearby diocese. He secured the last four places on the pilgrimage. They would be gone for seven days.

It was a warm day in June when Zélie and Léonie boarded the train for Le Mans. Marie had gone there a week before to attend an alumni retreat. After collecting the older girls, they would travel to Angers where the pilgrimage would start the next day. Léonie looked out the window all the way to Le Mans and talked frequently. She was very excited. Zélie was also excited and hopeful. *If it is God's plan, I will be cured; but regardless, I know it will be a good spiritual journey for us.*

Marie and Pauline were waiting at the convent. Upon Zélie and Léonie's arrival, the Visitation Sisters insisted on feeding them a delicious lunch. As they prepared to depart, Zélie was told that the whole community was praying for her.

"Thank you very much," Zélie said to the extern sister who was waiting on them.

"Is there anything you might need on the pilgrimage that we could give you?"

"I seem to have forgotten the container with water for us to drink. Do you have one I may borrow? Otherwise, I will buy one in Angers."

"Don't buy one. We have a very handy one. I will fill it for you."

The sister soon returned with the water container and handed it to Pauline. Then they all said their good-byes, and the Martins climbed into the waiting carriage.

They had not gone far when Pauline exclaimed, "Mama, the container is leaking!"

She gave the container to her mother. It was definitely dripping.

"Marie, lean out and tell the driver to return to the convent. We must take this back."

Upon Marie's request the driver turned back to the convent. Marie jumped out of the carriage and ran to the door. She rang the bell.

"Marie, you're back!" the extern sister exclaimed upon opening the door.

Marie thrust the water container on the surprised sister. "It's leaking." Then she ran back to the carriage, leaving the sister standing there speechless and getting wet.

The Martins made it to the train station with only a few minutes to spare. Soon they were on the train for Angers.

Pauline smiled. "Mama, remember the time Papa, Marie, and I were not paying attention on the train and missed our transfer?"

"I certainly do. I had prepared a lovely dinner, and it got cold awaiting you."

Zélie made sure the girls were ready to disembark as soon as they saw the first houses of Angers. "An extern sister from the Visitation Convent is supposed to meet us at the station. She will bring us to our hotel and then the convent. Sister Marie-Paula arranged this."

Pauline beamed. "It will be wonderful to see her again. I have missed her as headmistress."

A smiling extern sister was waiting for them on the platform in Angers. "You must be the Martin family," she said.

The sister brought them to the hotel and then to the convent. Marie and Pauline were overjoyed to see their beloved friend Sister Marie-Paula. Léonie stood by bored while her two sisters and Sister Marie-Paula engaged in happy conversation. It was late when they finally left the convent.

"It is nice that the extern sister is going on the pilgrimage too," Pauline remarked, holding on to the new water container just given them by the convent.

"Yes," Zélie responded, exhausted. "We must try to get to bed quickly, since the pilgrimage leaves at seven fifty tomorrow morning."

The next morning Zélie was ready to leave before any of her daughters, so she went to fill the new water container. The hotel manager showed her the way to the pump.

"If you need anything else, just tell me."

Zélie started to fill the container. It was taking a long time. She looked beneath it. *I am holding another watering can! This time I will get a container from the hotel manager and not from another Visitation convent.*

The manager gave Zélie a bottle, and it did not leak!

The Martins joined the pilgrimage in ample time. Zélie found four seats for them on the train and stashed their luggage. Soon the train started moving.

"We're on our way to Lourdes!" Léonie exclaimed.

A fellow passenger smiled. "In twenty-four short hours we will be there."

Or twenty-four long hours, Zélie thought later that day. *All three girls said they were going to take care of me on this trip, and instead I am constantly taking care of them. No wonder I never liked traveling.*

"Mama, that speck of dust is still irritating my eye."

"Marie, try to make yourself cry. It will come out eventually."

"I wish I had an onion."

"Mama, when can we eat?"

"You ate just an hour ago, Pauline."

"Mama, my feet hurt."

"I know, Léonie, but what can I do about it?"

"I don't know."

"Look at your book or out the window. Try thinking of something else."

By nightfall Zélie was exhausted, but the jolting of the train kept her awake. She longingly gazed at the girls sleeping peacefully. Eventually, insomnia gave way to exhaustion, and Zélie fell asleep. She was in the middle of a dream when she felt a tremendous force land on her. "Help!" she yelled, awaking abruptly.

The force had left and was walking toward the door. "Léonie, stop sleepwalking!" Zélie exclaimed.

Léonie promptly fell against the closed door and awoke.

"What's happening?" a passenger exclaimed.

"Are you all right?" another pilgrim inquired.

Everybody in their compartment was now awake. After making sure Léonie was fine, Zélie made her take a different seat. By then everyone had heard what had brought about the commotion, and they were laughing heartily. Zélie, relieved that the other travelers were not angry at their abrupt awakening, sank into her seat. Léonie promptly fell asleep, but it was the end of sleep for Zélie that night.

The train arrived in Lourdes earlier than scheduled. *Oh dear*, Zélie thought, *it is too early to call on the priest who was supposed to get us lodging. I will probably have to find a hotel myself.* Zélie and the girls walked by the rectory. There was no sign of life, so they went to the nearby hotel. Zélie started talking with the hotel proprietor.

A voice came from behind Zélie. "Pardon me for intruding, but are you Madame Martin?"

Zélie turned to see a man in clerical garb. "Father Martignon?" she asked.

"Yes, at your service. I saw you and your daughters pass by my window a short time ago. You fit the description of the Martins. I have already reserved a room for you at a local convent."

The Martins followed Father Martignon to the convent, and he made sure everything was settled before departing. Once their luggage was deposited in the room, Zélie ordered food for her hungry daughters.

"Mama, aren't you going to eat?"

"Not now. I will go to the Grotto and the spring first. I'll eat later."

After the girls had eaten, the Martins walked to the Grotto. Zélie gazed at the rock formation in front of them where Our Lady had appeared to fourteen-year-old Bernadette. A beautiful statue replicating the apparition stood in the niche. The Blessed Virgin had said on one of her visits, "I am the Immaculate Conception." On another visit she had told Bernadette to dig. Bernadette, with her hands, had obeyed, and a little spring had gurgled to the surface. Since then many miracles had been reported. The lame had walked, and the blind had seen.

Mass was going to begin soon. Zélie and the girls found a place close to the altar. *Here I am in this blessed spot, and I am too tired to pray,* Zélie thought.

After Mass Zélie left the girls to entertain themselves while she went to the spring. The spring now flowed into a building, in which tubs had been built for people to submerge themselves. Zélie looked at the water. *Will I be cured? Others have been.*

Zélie touched the water with a finger. *Brr, the water is cold, even in June. Such a shame the Blessed Mother did not give us a hot spring.* Hesitantly, Zélie climbed down into the water.

~

Every day in Alençon, Louis and the little girls hoped for a telegram. If Zélie were cured, she would send them one. Every time the doorbell rang, they rushed to the door; each time they were disappointed.

The week passed, and Louis took the little girls to the station. They waited patiently in the summer evening. The train's arrival time came and went. They continued to wait.

"Look, the train is coming!" Thérèse shouted.

"Thérèse, hold Céline's hand. Don't get too close to the tracks."

The train approached. Through a window they could see Zélie, Marie, and Léonie. Pauline had been dropped off at school to finish her term. Zélie was smiling.

Louis looked at his wife. She had not been cured, and yet she was happy. He resolved to follow her example and try not to be sad. Louis smiled in return as he helped them off the train. The little girls wanted to give their mama and sisters hugs. The platform was almost empty before Louis had a chance to embrace his wife.

"Louis," Zélie said as they walked toward home, "I still believe I will be cured. In fact, I brought back three liters of Lourdes water."

"Papa, one of the containers Mama bought for the holy water leaked," Léonie told him. "It was our third leaky container on the trip."

"Oh dear."

"Yes," Marie said, sighing. "And if our dresses smell like coffee, it is because there were two women on the train who had a spirit stove to make coffee. The coffee spilled on us and all over our food. We had coffee-bread."

"At least we were already in black dresses," Zélie remarked. "But it was dangerous. They could have started a fire."

Louis looked at Zélie. "Did anything else go wrong?"

"Oh yes. I lost my rosary, the only thing I had from

my sister, and then Pauline lost her rosary, which had two medals on it from Élise."

"Pauline cried about her loss, but Mama didn't," Léonie said gravely.

"Mama's rosary was lost by me in the grocery store in Lourdes," Marie explained sadly. "We looked everywhere, but we couldn't find it."

"It just disappeared," Zélie said, shrugging. "And among other things, I fell down two steps while carrying a vase of water and strained my neck badly."

"Oh no!"

"It's all right. We received a lot of graces on the trip. The one hard thing will be to face all the disbelievers who heard I was going to Lourdes. They will be thinking, 'I told you so.' How much I wanted to show them a thing or two."

"God hasn't hidden Himself from them; they have shut their eyes. Even with another miracle they would probably not believe."

"Very true. I keep remembering Our Lady's words to Bernadette: 'I don't promise to make you happy in this world, but in the next.'"

13

LISIEUX

ZÉLIE DID NOT GET BETTER. Now her neck hurt as well, but she refused to be gloomy. Instead, she tried to cheer up her family and make everything as nice as possible for them. Marie started to manage the house and the lace business although they were no longer accepting new orders.

Louise had asked Zélie to let her continue working for them while she was ill. "If you are cured, I will leave; but if you aren't, you need someone to take care of you."

"True, I do need help. All right, you may stay while I am sick, but if I die, you must leave."

"I promise."

Zélie also had made Louis and Marie promise to fulfill her wish.

Pauline, at school, had decided to pray that she might suffer in place of her mother. Zélie gently scolded her in a letter. "You want to suffer and go to Heaven in my place, and I will be left in Purgatory preparing myself for Heaven! Do you want that for me? While you want to take on my sufferings, why don't you add on my sins and imperfections too?"

Léonie, meanwhile, having read a story of a saintly woman who offered her life for someone else, decided to pray that she might die in her mother's place.

"Léonie," Zélie kindly said, "if God has a better plan for me than healing me, I want it. I desire to be with you on earth, but I accept whatever happens."

"Well . . . I am going to do a novena for my intention."

Zélie wondered how long Léonie would even have this resolve. However, one morning Léonie came downstairs and announced to Marie that God had answered her prayers and that she was dying.

"What!"

"I feel sick."

Léonie's face was so solemn that it made Marie laugh. The younger girl was offended, and Zélie had to come to the rescue and console her crying daughter.

A short time later Léonie was back to her worldly self, certain that she needed a pair of tapestry slippers. Zélie amusedly reminded her of their previous conversation. "If you are going to die, the slippers will be a waste of money."

Léonie did not say anything, but Zélie was sure she was thinking that she would have time to wear them first.

At the end of July Isidore and Céline came to Alençon for several days, and Pauline came home on August 1. Pauline helped Marie manage the house. Céline and Thérèse were sent each day to Adolphe's house, where his wife watched them.

One day Marie shared an idea with Pauline as they were talking in the kitchen. "Let's plan a little surprise for Mama! We could have an award ceremony like our school gave us. Céline and Thérèse would enjoy it, and Mama and Papa would be so pleased. We can use our bedroom for the ceremony, so Mama doesn't have to walk down the stairs."

"Let's do it. It is always such a special occasion at school. We should decorate our room and make prizes. Céline and Thérèse can wear their new white dresses."

"I knew you would like the idea. Will you make the prizes while I decorate the room? You are so good at art, and I have a vision for the room. I will see if Léonie wants to participate."

"Perfect!" Pauline hurried up to her room. She gathered scraps of ribbon, her paint brushes, and some paint; then she went to the kitchen to make some glue.

Early the next morning Marie was in the garden picking flowers. She gathered the best roses and chose dainty periwinkle flowers on their long vines to complement them. Sitting on a bench, she started to make long garlands and wreaths with the vines, sticking the roses intermittently among the periwinkle flowers.

Léonie helped her carry in the floral arrangements, and together they hung them throughout the bedroom. Then they placed a carpet in the middle of the floor and set up two armchairs as if they were thrones for the guests of honor.

"It's beautiful!" Pauline declared as she came into the room and placed the prizes on a table.

"Now I had better help Mama come in here," Marie told her sisters. "Pauline, please make sure Céline and Thérèse are dressed."

Soon everyone was ready: Zélie and Louis were seated in the places of honor; Léonie was sitting on a chair next to her mother; and the little girls, in their white dresses, were standing in the hall with Pauline.

Marie, a dignified headmistress, began her speech. "The prize ceremony for the Visitation Convent of Saint Mary of Alençon will now begin. We are very proud of the significant progress of our two students this year. Marie-Céline Martin and Marie-Françoise-Thérèse Martin, please enter."

Céline and Thérèse marched into the room. They were beaming in anticipation. Pauline entered and handed Louis and Zélie the prizes.

Marie looked down at the piece of paper she was holding. Last night Pauline and she had made a report of the students' progress. She started to read it.

Zélie smiled at her girls as she listened; she was very pleased with the progress the little girls had made in their education. She thought of Thérèse's first letter, written just a few months ago—her little hand being guided to do it—and of Céline's writing and art. She considered the many times she had heard Marie explaining math problems to the girls. She looked at Louis; he had made sure the girls knew history and geography. She thought the longest about her little daughters' understanding of the Faith.

After Marie finished listing Céline's and Thérèse's accomplishments, Zélie and Louis handed out the prizes. Marie had made wreaths to be awarded also. Pauline placed them on the girls' curly heads. Céline and Thérèse were very pleased.

Afterward, Thérèse exclaimed, "Mama, see our beautiful prizes!" Thérèse happily clutched the pretty hand-decorated ribbons.

"They are beautiful! You have both been good students," Zélie said.

The little girls went to their bedroom to find a home

for the prizes. Zélie turned to Léonie and patted her hand. "I am very pleased with the progress you have made this year, and it pleases me more than any colorful ribbon or fancy wreath could."

Léonie hugged her and then went to play with her little sisters.

After Léonie had left, Zélie looked at her two oldest daughters. "Marie, you have been doing an exceptional job teaching your little sisters and managing the house. Pauline, you have been and will be a great help to your sisters. I know I can trust you two girls to help raise your younger sisters. Just be very gentle with Léonie. She needs a lot of guidance and kind correction. She needs to feel very loved."

"She is!" Marie and Pauline both exclaimed.

"Of course—but she needs to realize it, with your help. You are all very blessed to have such a wonderful father!"

Zélie's illness worsened. Louis, Marie, and Louise took excellent care of their patient. Louis would sit awake at night beside Zélie to help her. During the day, Zélie would sometimes insist he take the younger girls on an excursion. They would go to please her, but no one enjoyed it. Louis' fifty-fourth birthday, August 22, passed by very sadly.

On August 26 the priest came to give Zélie the Last Rites. The whole family gathered in the bedroom, praying. The next day Isidore and Céline came from Lisieux in response to a telegram.

On August 28, at twelve thirty in the morning, God

called Zélie to eternal life. She was only forty-five.

Louis gazed at Zélie's face. It was so peaceful now! Despite his tears, he kept recalling the words of the Blessed Mother at Lourdes: "I don't promise to make you happy in this world, but in the next." *She is finally happy; I am sure. She was such a wonderful woman . . . I will miss her so, so very much . . .* "Zélie, you'll have to pray for us."

The funeral was held the next day in the Church of Notre-Dame. Zélie's family and friends gathered to commend her soul to God. Many of Zélie's lace workers were there crying. She had been not just an employer to them but also a friend. Louis, in his grief, was touched by how much Zélie had meant to other people.

That evening Louis and his daughters sadly gathered in the sitting room. They all felt at a loss. Louise had been upstairs packing her bags to leave. She came into the room, her bags left in the hall, to say good-bye. She had already found a new job.

Louise looked at forlorn Céline and Thérèse. "You poor children, without a mother."

Céline promptly rushed to Marie, threw her arms around her, and declared, "You will be my mother now!"

Thérèse then ran to Pauline and hugged her. "You are my mother now!"

Léonie stood there, watching her little sisters, then she went to her father.

Louis put his arms around her. She returned the embrace.

"We have each other, right?" he said.

"Yes," she murmured.

The Martins had to try to resume daily life; it was very hard. Days later, Louis knelt in Notre-Dame praying for guidance. Family and friends were giving him suggestions for his daughters' futures. He had talked with Marie and Pauline. They had been unhelpful, their responses being only, "Whatever you think is best, Papa." Pauline had, however, said she no longer wanted to return to school. "I loved the school, but my place is now with my family."

But where was that place to be? Zélie had not said much to Louis about it, but he felt that she would want him to move the family to Lisieux so that Isidore and especially Céline would be there for the girls. Louis found Isidore to be strong and overbearing, but he had grown into a good, strong Catholic and a wise man. Céline was a kind, gentle woman, the perfect person to help his daughters. Louis was sure Zélie had never suggested the move because she thought it was too much to ask of him: his mother, friends, family gravesites—everything—was in Alençon. *But what matters*, Louis thought, *is what is best for my daughters*. He was rather sure that Marie and Pauline wanted to move to Lisieux, but like their mother they refrained from saying it. Isidore had invited him to move his family there. Only the word "yes" was needed, and Isidore would start looking for a house for the Martins.

Meanwhile, Madame Tifenne, Léonie's godmother, and Mademoiselle Romet, Pauline's godmother, had offered to take the older two girls and introduce them into society. "They are at the age now. We will make sure they get into good, moral groups." Louis' friends urged him to accept their generous offer and to place the younger girls in boarding school. "You are too old to have to be constantly watching out for them."

They are sure they know best, but I don't think so. Zélie wouldn't want it, and neither do I. We need to be together now. The girls feel that way, and as for Marie and Pauline coming out into society, neither of the girls has any interest in that. My daughters need good, wholesome friends. It does seem like we should move to Lisieux, to be closer to the Guérins. I will have to leave my mother, but I can come back often to visit her. "God, please help me to know if it is Your will that we move."

Louis conferred with the three older girls and told them he was thinking of moving to Lisieux. They were enthusiastic. *I know the answer: we are meant to move.* Louis sent the word to Isidore, "Yes, we are coming!"

Meanwhile, Louis was trying to sell the lace business. He would also sell the house, but he was going to keep the Pavilion. That way he would have a place to stay when he visited. His mother was not as strong as she once was. Adolphe was married with two children. Madame Martin needed more care than they could give. *Maybe Rose Taillé would be willing to have her live with them. They would get along well together, and I would not worry about my mother.*

A week later a letter arrived from Isidore. After looking at twenty-five houses for rent, he had found an excellent one. It had a garden and was secluded but was near the town and a nice size for the Martins. It was close to Isidore's house and even closer to the church.

"It sounds excellent!" Marie exclaimed.

"Definitely," Pauline added.

"I agree," Louis said. "Next week I will go to Lisieux to rent the house."

It was mid-November when the Martins were ready to move. Rose and her family had been happy to have Madame Martin move in with them; Louis had helped his mother move. There was still business for Louis to attend to in Alençon, so the girls left without him. By the end of the month, he had sold the lace business and was free to leave.

The girls met him at the station in Lisieux.

"Now, Papa, pretend you have never before seen Les Buissonnets. See what a nice place we have made of it," Pauline told him.

"Les Buissonnets. What a pretty name!"

Marie smiled and said, "We adapted the neighborhood's name to make it sound better and named the house after its location."

Les Buissonnets was set off the main road and behind a park. A stony path, entered by a beautiful gate, ran up a steep hill to the three-story house surrounded by shrubs. The top floor had a steep roof and beautiful dormer windows.

"Come inside, Papa!" the five girls said.

They eagerly showed him the elegant wood-paneled dining room, the kitchen, and the sitting room. Then he was led upstairs and shown his bedroom and the other bedrooms. One was for Marie and Pauline, one for Léonie, and one for Céline and Thérèse. The girls seemed to be getting more excited by the moment.

"Now for the attic!" Marie headed for the stairs.

Louis knew that on the top floor there were three small rooms and one larger room with a fireplace. He wondered at their excitement.

"See, Papa!"

Louis looked around the large room. It was furnished plainly, with an armchair, a table, and a bookshelf. He looked at the books. "These are all my books!"

"Yes, Papa," Marie said. "We thought this could be your new Pavilion. It is called the Belvedere. You will be able to read and pray here in peace."

Louis was very touched by his daughters' thoughtfulness. "Thank you so much!"

The next morning Thérèse insisted on showing Louis where she thought her new swing should go. "It's the perfect place!" she exclaimed, pointing to a place in the backyard near a shed. "I like this garden better than the front one. There are so many surprise places!"

Louis had to agree. This garden had winding paths

and tall trees. There was a place to grow a vegetable garden, and a nice flower bed. *Zélie always wanted us to have a bigger garden. She got her wish,* Louis realized.

Although Louis missed Alençon, Lisieux quickly became home for the girls. In January Léonie and Céline were enrolled at the nearby Benedictine convent school. Pauline gave Thérèse her lessons at home. They employed a maid whose name was Victoire. The Guérin daughters, Jeanne and Marie, became playmates to Céline and Thérèse, and Marie and Pauline greatly appreciated their aunt Céline's help and advice. Léonie, with her family's loving help, was overcoming her difficulties and managing better in school. Louis bought chickens, ducks, and rabbits. He made an aviary for pet birds and an aquarium for Thérèse's goldfish.

Every few months Louis traveled to Alençon to visit his mother and friends. In the summer he took Marie and Pauline to Paris for the World's Fair. They witnessed electric lights suddenly flooding the streets around the Opera House. The night had never been so bright. They saw the phonograph and the megaphone: inventions of Thomas Edison, an American. There was another new invention, something one could speak into and the sound would be transmitted and come out another device a distance away: it was called the telephone. Louis, walking among the displays of thirty-six countries from around the world, dreamed of traveling again. They saw a colossal sculpture of a woman's face, big enough for people to walk inside, named Liberty.

It would be a part of a huge statue to be sent to the United States as a gift. While in Paris, the Martins also visited Our Lady of Victories Church and the Cathedral of Notre-Dame. Finally restored, the cathedral was magnificent.

Lisieux was placid compared with Alençon. In the mornings the Martins would attend the early weekday Mass, and then they would spend their morning doing housework or their lessons. In the afternoons Louis would take Thérèse on walks along quiet paths and to churches. She eagerly looked forward to these excursions with her papa, whom she called "my King," since she was his "Little Queen." Louis had nicknames for all of his daughters: Marie was "my Diamond," or "the Gypsy," because of her independent spirit. Pauline was "the Fine Pearl." Léonie was "Good-Hearted Léonie," and Céline was "the Dauntless One." In the evenings the family would gather in the sitting room, where they played checkers. Often someone would read a book aloud.

Louis and Isidore organized nocturnal Adoration in Lisieux. Louis joined the Conference of Saint Vincent de Paul. The Martins continued to be very generous to the poor and needy. On Mondays the family ran a little soup kitchen at their house.

~

One day Louis and Céline were walking home. Opposite Les Buissonnets was a little hut where a poor Irish family lived. Today there was a strange smell of smoke in the air.

"Stay here, Céline!" Louis ordered, hurrying toward the hut.

Looking through the open door, Louis saw an elderly woman trying to put out a fire with a leaky bucket. Louis glanced around outside. There was a battered, rusty water pump nearby. Louis ran to it while taking off his coat and hat. He soaked the coat with water and filled the hat; then he rushed back to the hut.

The elderly woman was hobbling out of her house.

Louis hurried inside. He threw his wet coat on the flames. Then he dumped the water in his hat over his coat. The elderly woman appeared with more water in her leaky bucket. Louis took the water and doused his coat again. Soon he had the fire smothered.

The woman started to thank him in her foreign language. Louis smiled and nodded at her. Then he picked up his coat and hat and returned to Céline. The girls would be worried about them.

~

Another day Louis went fishing. He had found a lovely stream: it meandered its way through deserted meadows. Climbing a stone wall to get to it, Louis walked along the creek before depositing his fishing box near a calm pool. *This is the perfect spot!* Louis placed his poles on the ground and prepared to cast his line.

Suddenly he heard a noise; he turned. A bull was charging straight toward him! Louis grabbed his poles and started running for his life. The wall seemed so far away!

He heard a smash. *There goes my fishing box!* He glanced behind him—the bull was still coming; he was never going to make it! Louis threateningly waved his poles at the bull. The animal drew back a little. Louis started running again. The bull was following once more. Louis turned and waved his poles again. It was working! He was gaining distance!

The wall was right in front of him now! He took a flying leap and landed on the other side . . . safe! He could hear his enemy snorting about his loss.

He lay there catching his breath. "Thank You, God, for helping me." After the shock wore off, he got to his feet, picked up his poles, and headed home. *I've had enough fishing for today!*

14

LOUIS' OFFERINGS

ONE MORNING IN THE EARLY SPRING of 1882, twenty-year-old Pauline came to find Louis, who was reading in the Belvedere.

"Papa, I would like to talk with you."

"Yes, my Pearl." Louis put down his book. "What is it?"

"Papa, for years I have had a strong desire to become a nun. I always thought I was called to the Visitation order like my aunt, but just recently I have felt that my call is to Carmel, to the monastery in this town."

"To Carmel?" Louis was dazed by this sudden announcement. He had known for years that his Pearl had a strong desire for the religious life, but he was always sure she would enter the Visitation Convent in Le Mans. "Pauline, the Carmelite rule is very austere."

"I know. I want it. With your permission, I would like to arrange a visit with the mother superior to talk about entering."

Pauline left the room to give her father time to contemplate the news.

Later that day Louis met her alone on the stairs. He hesitated a moment before speaking. "Pauline, dear . . . I give you permission to talk with the superior, and to enter Carmel if that should indeed be your call. But know it is no small sacrifice on my part . . . I love you very dearly."

"Thank you, Papa!" Pauline exclaimed, hugging him. "I love you very dearly too. You wanted to become a monk, so you can understand how I long to give myself totally to God."

On October 2, 1882, Pauline entered Carmel. Although her family was happy for her, she was sorely missed, especially by nine-year-old Thérèse. After Zélie's death, Thérèse had changed from a happy little girl to a crying, shy, and sensitive child who was content only with her family and cousins. Within the last year, after Léonie's graduation, Thérèse had begun studies at the

Benedictine school. Pauline's departure was one more change, and Thérèse was taking it hard.

For Holy Week 1883 Louis decided to take Marie and Léonie to Paris while Céline and Thérèse stayed with the Guérins. They went to the Cathedral of Notre-Dame on Holy Thursday. Louis found the packed cathedral very inspiring. They visited other important places in the city, but as always, Our Lady of Victories was Louis' favorite. A Jesuit priest, Father Pichon, who was Marie's spiritual director, was in the city. Louis and Léonie met him, and they all became friends.

On Easter Monday, early in the morning, they received a telegram with bad news. Thérèse was sick. Quickly they packed their luggage and boarded the next train for Lisieux.

When they arrived, they found Thérèse violently sick with convulsions, anorexia, and hallucinations. The doctor and Isidore were very concerned and somewhat puzzled. Thérèse's incoherent ramblings were focused on Pauline, who was going to take the habit shortly and would become Sister Agnès of Jesus. Thérèse begged to be allowed to go to the ceremony, but she was too sick to leave her uncle's house.

On the morning of the clothing ceremony, Thérèse got up and declared she was cured. She was able to visit Pauline and then go back home.

Early the next morning Louis was awoken by Léonie. "Papa, get the doctor! Thérèse is worse than ever!"

The doctor's treatments were useless. Thérèse now

lay in Marie's room, her symptoms worse than before. Louis, meanwhile, got the sad news that his mother had died; it could not have come at a worse moment. He traveled to Alençon by himself—the girls staying with Thérèse—and returned home as fast as possible.

Everyone was praying ardently. Near Thérèse's bed on a chest stood the Martins' statue of the Blessed Virgin. They would kneel before the statue, pleading to God for Thérèse. Louis sent a request to his beloved Our Lady of Victories Church for a novena of Masses for her. He kept thinking, *She is so like my little Hélène!* "Please, God, leave her with us."

On Pentecost Louis returned to church in the afternoon to pray. He felt helpless. He walked home slowly, thinking of Thérèse. "Zélie, please ask God to heal her."

Marie met him at the door. "Thérèse is cured!" she exclaimed.

"She is? Really?" Louis could barely believe his ears.

"I know she is, this time for good! She was delirious, and Léonie, Céline, and I were all kneeling by her bedside, praying. Thérèse was saying, 'Mama! Mama!' as she gazed at the Blessed Virgin statue. Then tears came into her eyes, and her face was filled with joy. She was in ecstasy for three or four minutes, and now she is fine! The Blessed Mother cured her!"

Marie related to her father what Thérèse had told her. "The statue was suddenly so beautiful! The Blessed

Virgin's face was alive with love, and she smiled, the most beautiful smile ever, at Thérèse. And then Thérèse felt her pain disappear!"

"The Blessed Mother has given us a miracle!" Louis declared gratefully.

To regain her strength, Thérèse did not go back to school for months. In the late summer Louis took his family to Alençon. It was the first time that Thérèse and Céline had returned to the town since moving to Lisieux.

Louis' friends were delighted to see the two younger girls after so many years. Mademoiselle Pauline Romet and Madame Tifenne planned parties and fun excursions for the Martin girls. Louis took them to visit Rose Taillé and to see his mother's grave, and they made multiple trips to Zélie's grave. Louis watched his daughters kneel in front of the stone and thought of how Zélie had never really left him: he still felt her presence when he prayed.

On one of the days Léonie asked if they could visit the Poor Clare Monastery.

"Certainly," Louis responded.

Since Marie was visiting with friends, and Céline and Thérèse had been taken horseback riding, Louis and Léonie went alone. Louis had gone fishing that morning, and he brought some of his catch with them. "This reminds me of years ago, before I married your mother. I would spend my holidays fishing and deposit my catch with the Poor Clares," Louis told Léonie. "Once I was married and had children, my children wanted to eat my catch."

Léonie smiled. "I like visiting the Poor Clares because Mama would take me there on walks with her. I told her once to ask them to pray for me that I might become a nun. You know, I do want to someday."

"Yes," Louis said, nodding at his twenty-year-old. He was sure that Léonie would persevere toward her dream, but she needed more time at home to prepare. Many of her ideas were passing dreams, but this one was not.

That evening an excited Marie informed her family that Father Pichon was in town and that he desired to meet the youngest two Martins. They had planned a small party for Louis' birthday, and they invited Father Pichon to attend. They all liked the kind priest. He, in turn, was impressed and felt welcomed by the family.

As the year passed, Louis watched his children continue to grow up. Thérèse had her First Holy Communion, and on the same day, May 8, 1884, Pauline, now Sister Agnès, made her solemn profession. The following month Thérèse was confirmed with Léonie as her sponsor.

Soon after Thérèse's Confirmation, Louis decided to fulfill one of her long-desired wishes. "Thérèse, come out to the garden," he called.

Thérèse ran out the door. Her face lit up upon seeing Louis' surprise. "A dog! What a beautiful spaniel! Papa, is he for me? What is his name?"

"He is for you. You can name him."

Thérèse knelt down and held the frisky fellow. She looked him in the eyes and said, "I think Tom would be a good name for you."

Tom looked forward to his afternoon walks as eagerly as Thérèse did. Louis always accompanied them. On one of their excursions, the playful puppy ran into a mud puddle. His beautiful fur became matted and ugly.

"See?" Louis said to Thérèse, "Tom's fur is ugly now. He needs to be washed. So it is with our souls; when we get ourselves in the puddles of sin, we need to be washed clean in confession."

~

One day a priest friend, Father Charles-Marie, approached Louis. "I am taking a pilgrimage to various cities in Europe. I know you love traveling and was wondering if you would join me. We would be gone about two and a half months."

"That is a long time to leave my daughters, but it does sound wonderful."

"Talk it over with your daughters."

"I will."

Marie, after Pauline's encouragement, overcame her

objections and urged him to go. "This is your chance! We will be all right without you."

Her sisters agreed with her.

Louis went. He visited Paris, Munich, Vienna, Budapest, Varna, Constantinople, Athens, Naples, Rome, and Milan. It was wonderful. He had only two disappointments: they had to give up the idea of visiting the Holy Land because of a lack of transportation, and they were not able to see the pope.

~

Louis was very glad to be reunited with his daughters after his long trip. He had missed them greatly.

Several months later Marie came to Louis with a matter of importance. "I feel God is calling me to the Carmelites."

Louis sighed; his heart was heavy. "But . . . without you . . ."

"Papa, Céline is seventeen. She is old enough to run the house. Everything will be fine; you will see."

"God could not ask for a greater sacrifice. I never thought you would leave me." Louis tried to conceal his tears as he embraced his eldest.

~

Before Marie entered Carmel, she wanted her father to take her to Calais. Father Pichon, who had been in

Canada for two years, was returning to France. His ship would dock in Dublin, Ireland, and he would take a boat to Dover, England, and then another one to Calais, France. Marie wanted to see him and thought that the easiest way would be to go to Calais. Louis consented to her plan.

After waiting two days in Calais for Father Pichon, Louis suggested they travel to Dover to try to meet him. They boarded a ferry. Slowly the coast of France faded into the distance. Marie watched the horizon in anticipation. Louis, listening to the various languages being spoken around them, thought of his recent trip to eastern Europe. His voyages on the Black Sea and the Mediterranean Sea had had calmer waves than the English Channel, and he felt fortunate not to be seasick. This would be his first time to visit England.

"Look, Papa!" Marie exclaimed. "There is a white line on the horizon."

"It must be the white cliffs of Dover. They are made of chalky stone and are glistening in the sunlight."

When the boat docked, Louis took Marie to a restaurant. Louis enjoyed the different architecture and landscape, but Marie was intimidated by the bustling port and was interested only in the reason for their visit, seeing Father Pichon. After eating, Louis found a place for them to wait on the dock.

Hours passed by, and Father Pichon still had not appeared. Louis went to ask authorities about the priest's boat, but they shook their heads: they did not seem to know about the boat. As Marie became more and more discouraged, Louis tried to cheer her.

"Don't worry, Marie. If we don't see Father Pichon here, we can see him in Paris on our way home. That is where he is supposed to end up, and we will try to find him. There must be some mistake about arrival times. We should probably go to our hotel now."

"I am so annoyed at myself for making you take this trip for nothing."

"Don't be, Marie. God has allowed this to happen for some good reason. I am happy to be His instrument in making this trip with you."

The next day there was still no boat from Dublin. Louis and Marie boarded the ferry and returned to France. They went to Paris and found Father Pichon. There had indeed been a miscommunication, and the priest was very apologetic.

Louis smiled. "That happens; it is all right. Marie and I got to see a new place and practice patience."

Marie listened sheepishly to the last statement.

~

Marie also requested they take a family trip to Alençon. She wanted to pray at her mother's grave one last time. Meanwhile, Léonie visited the Poor Clare Monastery again. She still had her dream of entering the convent, and she decided to talk with the nuns about it.

Afterward she told Louis about her visit while the

other girls were out visiting friends. "Papa, you know I have always wanted to be a nun. I asked the Poor Clares if I could join them. They said yes! I told them that I wanted to join them now!"

"Now?"

"Yes. Why waste time? I will miss you all, but I am so excited to be a nun that I want to join immediately."

It was hard for Louis to explain to his other daughters that Léonie would not be coming home with them. They were all stunned, and Marie was very displeased.

"How can she run off and desert you all of a sudden! She will be so far away from you all. She didn't even say good-bye to Pauline or our relatives."

"Léonie has always been impulsive, but she does everything for good reasons," Louis told them. "Don't be mad at her. She has wanted to be a religious since she was little, probably longer than Pauline wanted to be a nun."

"That is true, Papa," Marie agreed. "I will try not to be mad at her."

Her sisters echoed her words.

~

On October 15, 1886, Marie entered Carmel. On December 1, less than two months after entering the Poor Clare Monastery, Léonie returned home, sick.

"They told me that I am not strong enough to be a Poor Clare."

"It is all right," Louis said, embracing her. "I am glad to have you home for now. There are plenty of other orders. Get well and pray about it. God will show you the way."

~

Louis was unusually tired that Christmas Eve. The family went to Midnight Mass as was their custom. Upon arriving home, Louis almost stumbled over a pair of shoes in front of the fireplace. The shoes were laden with presents that were for almost-fourteen-year-old Thérèse.

"Thankfully, this is the last year we will have this kind of thing," Louis blurted aloud to himself. As soon as he had said it, he regretted his hasty remark. *Oh no. Thérèse will cry if she heard that.* He could hear Céline upstairs and Thérèse climbing the stairs.

Several minutes later Thérèse came into the room. She was all smiles. Céline was following her, a worried look on her face. Thérèse started to open the packages, happily exclaiming over each little item. She soon had Louis laughing over her remarks. Céline watched the proceedings, stunned.

Little did Louis realize that Thérèse had indeed heard his comment and that he was witnessing what Thérèse was to call her "Christmas miracle": the night she regained the composure and cheerfulness she had lost when her mother died. What Louis did realize in the days that followed was that Thérèse was no longer given to crying and was now very motivated in educating herself. She had been taken out of school and was having lessons with a tutor, but her thirst for education drove her to pursue studies on her own also. She was very interested in history and science.

Even as Thérèse was changing, so was Louis. In early May he had a slight stroke; he recovered, but his health was no longer good. For the first time in his sixty-four years, he felt old.

On Pentecost Louis sat in the garden, watching the sunset and contemplating God's love. Four years ago Thérèse had been miraculously cured on this great feast.

Thérèse came out of the house and toward him. She had become a beautiful little woman who found innocent delight in everything. Today, though, she walked as if something was weighing on her mind. She had traces of tears in her eyes.

"What is it, my Little Queen? Tell me." Louis stood up and clasped her hand. They walked together through the garden.

"Papa, I want to enter Carmel, and I want to enter soon."

Tears came into Louis' eyes—another child for him to give to God. "You are very young to make such a serious decision."

"Yes, but Jesus said, 'Let the little children come to me' and 'Unless you turn and become like little children, you will not enter into the kingdom of heaven.' I am a child, and at what better place can Jesus play with me than Carmel? I want to give myself totally to Jesus and live completely for Him. I want to enter Carmel especially to spend time in prayer that souls may find God. I want to become a fisher of souls! No sacrifice is too great for one's beloved."

Louis led Thérèse to a low wall along the garden path. He reached down to pick a small white flower; its roots remained unbroken. "Once there was a little seed that was planted in a sheltered spot. Gentle rain and soft sunlight nurtured it until it started to blossom forth. Then the flower was plucked and planted again so that it could live in more fertile soil." Louis gave the flower to Thérèse.

Thérèse's eyes were shining. She hugged her father. She knew that she was the little flower, and he had just given her permission to fulfill her heart's desire.

In happy silence, Thérèse looked down at the small flower. She would put it in a book to press it. She would always have it.

That summer Léonie entered the Visitation Convent in Caen, and Louis reserved places on a pilgrimage to Italy in October for his two youngest daughters and himself. He wanted to give Céline and Thérèse the opportunity to see many of the great sights. Thérèse, meanwhile, asked the ecclesiastical superior of Carmel for acceptance; her dream was to enter on the first anniversary of her Christmas miracle.

The ecclesiastical superior of Carmel said Thérèse

could not enter until she was twenty-one, but he added, "I am only the bishop's deputy. Ask the bishop."

Louis and Thérèse went to see the bishop. The vicar-general for the diocese, Father Révérony, arranged the meeting.

The bishop seemed quite surprised that Louis would want to fulfill his daughter's desire. *Doesn't a good father try to answer his child's request?* Louis reflected afterward. *And how could I not want to fulfill her wish, even though it is a great sacrifice for me to make? She is a treasure God lent me to cherish and nourish, and now He wants her for Himself.*

"I will give you my answer while you are in Italy," the bishop decided.

Three days later the Martins boarded a train for Paris. They would see some of the principal sites of the city before starting the pilgrimage. They rode along the famous street Champs-Élysées; passed underneath the Arc de Triomphe; visited the Louvre and the Opera House; took a ride in an elevator; and visited churches. Céline was enthralled with the art she saw. For Thérèse the most important site was Our Lady of Victories Church; like Louis, she found great peace there. The day before the pilgrimage was to start, the 197 pilgrims met for Mass at Sacré-Cœur, which was still being built.

The pilgrimage departed early the next morning. Unlike the Martins, many of the pilgrims were nobility or priests, Father Révérony being one of them. Each compartment on their train was named after a saint. The Martins were assigned to Saint Martin; it became a joke on the train to call Louis "Monsieur Saint Martin"!

When the train ride took them through Switzerland, Céline and Thérèse pressed their noses to the glass and marveled at the magnificent views. Louis reflected on his previous longing to join the monks at the Great Saint Bernard Pass; he was very glad he had been called to marriage and blessed with Zélie and their children. *God's plan was far better than I could have imagined.*

In Italy they visited Milan, Venice, Padua, Bologna, Loreto, and Rome. Louis enjoyed showing his two youngest the Eternal City. As usual, Céline and Thérèse were their independent selves. In Loreto they had insisted on attending Mass in the Holy House from Nazareth instead of going to the pilgrimage Mass celebrated on the basilica's main altar. Now in Rome, they were dismayed that visitors were not taken into the excavated arena of the Colosseum, where they were told so many martyrs had shed their blood for Christ.

The tour group was being shown around the edge of the arena when Thérèse exclaimed to Céline, "Come on, follow me. We can do it!"

Both girls began clambering over the ruins.

"Céline, Thérèse, come back!" Louis shouted. It was useless; their hearts were set on reaching the place.

Louis watched them. Upon reaching the arena floor, they knelt down, prayed, and kissed the ground.

Later that day when they were in the catacombs, the

girls lay down where Saint Cecilia's incorrupt body once had been. Louis decided there was no reason to scold them; if he had been young and able, he would have done it also. *I am grateful that this is what is so important to them.*

On their last day in Rome, the pilgrims attended Mass celebrated by the pope, Leo XIII, in his chapel. Later that day there was an audience with him. Each pilgrim in the group would be presented, kneel, and receive a blessing. Father Révérony would present them. When Louis' turn came, Father Révérony introduced him as "the father of two Carmelite nuns and a Visitation Sister." The pope laid his hand on Louis' head and gave him a special blessing. Louis left the room with an indescribable sense of peace.

Céline and Thérèse were a distance behind Louis in the line. He was very surprised when they caught up with him to see Thérèse visibly upset.

"Whatever is the matter, Thérèse?"

"Papa, right before my turn, Father Révérony said that we were not to speak to the Holy Father. But I did! I said I had a great favor to ask of him in honor of his jubilee: could I enter Carmel at fourteen? Then Father Révérony interrupted me and said the authorities are looking into the matter. The Holy Father told me, 'Very well, my child, do whatever they say.' The guards wanted me to leave, but I needed the Holy Father to understand that if he said yes, then everyone else would consent!"

"Yes, Thérèse."

"He told me I would enter if God wills it."

"Thérèse, don't be dismayed. That is the answer! You will enter if it is God's will. He can change people's hearts. Remember that what is most important is to do God's will, to do it willingly, and to do it well."

"Yes, Papa."

The next day, most of the pilgrims, including Céline and Thérèse, traveled to Naples and Pompeii. Louis remained in Rome. He wanted to visit a religious brother he had met on his previous trip. He was very surprised when Father Révérony also came to see the brother. Louis and Father Révérony had a good talk about Thérèse's desire to enter Carmel and her experience at the papal audience. The vicar-general explained that he had been trying to speed up the audience since the frail pope was obviously very tired. Louis ascertained that Father Révérony appreciated Thérèse's request and that he could be influential with the bishop. The bishop had sent word recently that he was not going to give an answer while they were in Italy.

After Rome and Naples, the pilgrims went to Assisi. It was a beautiful, peaceful change from bustling Rome. Then it was onward to Florence, Pisa, Geneva, Nice, Marseille, Lyon, and finally Paris. This time the Martins did not stay over in the capital; they were eager to get home. They had been gone for almost a month.

Thérèse's dream was to enter on the anniversary of

her Christmas miracle. She wrote letters but to no avail. Louis and Céline kept reminding her to abandon herself to God's will: in due time she would surely enter. Christmas Day came, and no answer had been given. Céline gave Thérèse a little boat with the word *abandonment* painted on it to remind her that someday she would arrive at her desired port. Louis treasured every moment he had with his youngest.

On New Year's Day Thérèse received a letter. The bishop had granted her request! However, Carmel had decided she should wait to enter until after the Lenten fast. Louis offered to take Thérèse on a pilgrimage to the Holy Land to make the wait more bearable, but she declined; she wanted to prepare herself at home. Only a few days later, Louis had to travel to Caen; Léonie, not being able to adjust to life at the convent, was returning home.

"Don't be discouraged," Louis told Léonie. "We all have our disappointments. You can always try again."

"I know, but I have so many failings," Léonie said sadly.

"The things in life that we think prevent us from being saints are the very things that can make us saints."

"That is very true." Léonie was silent for a moment, thinking. "Papa, I guess I should not be discouraged by my failings."

"Indeed, it is by our failings that we realize how much we need God."

"And then those things in life that we think keep us from God are our crosses, and we have a choice to embrace them or reject them."

"That's it. Exactly."

~

Louis thought about how he could help Thérèse prepare for her entrance. He decided to buy her a pet lamb: nurturing the animal would help her understand how God was nurturing her. On Ash Wednesday he gave the gentle creature to her.

She knelt on the ground holding its trembling little body. "Papa, he is the perfect gift for me. I understand what you mean. I will cherish caring for him this spring." She knew that upon her departure, Céline and her papa would enjoy the new pet, just as they would enjoy Tom.

Thérèse and Céline cared for the lamb tenderly that day, but in the afternoon, the little creature was not well. "What do you think is the matter with our lamb?" Thérèse asked her father.

He bent over the little, white, fluffy animal. "I do not know. Maybe he got too cold before coming here."

The lamb died that day. Thérèse sadly held the little animal in her lap. She stroked the lifeless creature.

"I am so sorry, Thérèse," Louis told her. "The poor little lamb . . . I can buy you another one."

"No thank you, Papa. He was an excellent reminder for me that only in Heaven will we be truly content."

The day came, April 9, 1888, when Louis escorted Thérèse to Carmel. His heart was heavy but peaceful. *I shall miss her, but I am grateful that I have a gift to give God.*

Several weeks later Louis was kneeling in the Church of Notre-Dame in Alençon. He thought of how, almost thirty years ago, he and Zélie had gotten married there; fifteen years ago his Little Queen had been baptized in the building; and eleven years ago Zélie's funeral had been in it. For years they had worshiped there. As he was praying, he felt God's presence so strongly that his love for God seemed completely inadequate. He gazed at the crucifix: Jesus' arms were outstretched on the cross out of love. *I love You so much, Jesus, but it is nothing compared to Your immense love for me. You suffered so much; I want to join in Your suffering.*

~

One day in mid-June, Céline came into Louis' room. She was clad in her painter's smock and held a canvas.

"Papa," she said, smiling, "I have a gift for you!" She showed him the painting.

It was a painting of Saint Mary Magdalen looking up at the comforting face of Our Lady of Sorrows. Louis gazed at it. "Céline, it is beautiful! It looks so real."

"Oh, thank you. I am so glad you like it."

"I certainly do. You have such talent!" Louis was silent for a moment, thinking about Céline's future. He wondered what she actually wanted to do in life, since recently she had turned down a marriage proposal. "Céline, I am willing to take you to Paris so you can apprentice at a professional art studio."

"Thank you, Papa, but no thank you. To tell you the truth, I also want to become a Carmelite, but I will not ask for entrance until you no longer need me. Thérèse and I decided I would stay with you."

Louis took Céline's hand. "God be praised!" Tears came to his eyes. "Let us go to the Blessed Sacrament and pray, thanking God for the graces he has bestowed on our family. Someday all five of my daughters on earth will be brides of Christ, for I know Léonie will persevere and someday be a Visitation Sister!"

~

In May 1883, five years before Thérèse entered Carmel, Louis had his first stroke; he subsequently had two more. His physical and mental health were both impaired. He considered becoming a hermit. His days of dreaming about being a monk at the Great Saint Bernard Pass were gone, but he thought he could manage being a hermit. Céline would not need to worry about him. He impulsively decided to go to Le Havre to deal with business. Four days later a very worried Céline and Isidore located him there. He had forgotten to tell them his plans. Then the day came when Louis found his favorite parakeet dead because he had forgotten to feed it. *I am getting old and sick.* "I accept it, God. May I still glorify You."

Louis was upset when other people did not seem to know things he thought were obvious. He sometimes thought that his country was at war and the enemy was coming to attack. Scared that irreligious authorities were after the convents, he would set out on trips to protect his daughters. Eventually, someone would find him and bring him home. Acquaintances made fun of his confusion, and his family worried about him.

Finally Louis was told by his family that he could no longer live safely in his own house. Louis bravely accepted their decision. A friend took him to a home for the ill and elderly in Caen. Céline and Léonie visited him as often as possible. Louis accepted his new life and found joy in it: he could still go to daily Mass, spend time in prayer, and even help other residents. He was always sharing whatever his daughters gave him with other patients.

Then Louis had more strokes and became paralyzed. His daughters brought him back to Lisieux. The lease on Les Buissonnets had ended, so Isidore rented a house near his for the Martins. Meanwhile, Céline hired a married couple, Desiré and Marie; Desiré cared for Louis while Marie tended to the housework. Louis spent many hours in his wheelchair in the garden admiring nature or inside listening to his niece Marie play music. He was a very good patient.

One day Céline and Léonie took Louis to Carmel. Marie, Pauline, and Thérèse were there smiling—Louis was very happy to see them. He longed to be able to tell them how much he loved and cared about them, but he was unable, since his ill health made it difficult to speak. They did all the talking. At the end of the stay, Louis raised his hand and, in a voice choked with happy tears, said, "Heaven." His daughters would all know how much he meant in that simple word and that he was looking forward to someday being with them in their eternal home.

In the summer Louis was taken to a country residence that Céline Guérin had inherited. Louis enjoyed being pushed through the peaceful woodlands and meadows. Céline was his tender companion; Léonie had decided to try joining the Visitation Sisters again. The following summer Louis and Céline returned to the country house.

It was there on July 29, 1894, that God called Louis to Himself. Céline, crying, knelt beside his bed. Even though her heart was sad, she felt an incredible sense of joy. Her father's longing for God was finally fulfilled.

EPILOGUE

Little would Louis and Zélie have guessed as they made their marriage vows, that their own youthful dreams, transplanted by God, would bear much universal fruit. All five Martin children who lived to adulthood would persevere in the religious life, living the dream Louis and Zélie had had for their own lives. Thérèse would be canonized in 1925, only twenty-eight years after her death. Her autobiography, *Story of a Soul*, written in Carmel at the request of Marie and Pauline, would make Thérèse known worldwide. She would be proclaimed patroness of foreign missions, and patroness of France along with Saint Joan of Arc. Many a soldier during World War I said he owed his life to Thérèse's intercession, and many men were inspired to become priests after reading about Thérèse's life and her zeal for saving souls. Thérèse would be declared a Doctor of the Church because of her significant contribution to the Church's understanding of God's love. Her four sisters, three as Carmelites and one as a Visitation nun, would spend their lives practicing and promulgating Thérèse's "Little Way," the path of living the ordinary for God.

But surely what would have surprised Louis and Zélie the most was that their names would be taken to Rome as candidates for sainthood, and on October 18, 2015, they would become the first married couple to be canonized together. They would be known as Saints Louis and Zélie Martin.

AUTHOR'S NOTE

Saint Thérèse has always had a special place in my life. She is also important to my mother, who prayed to her for a child. I am that child. I do not recall first hearing about the Little Flower; it is as if she has always been there for me as a great friend and model. I had my First Holy Communion on her feast day, and I took her for my Confirmation saint. When Vivian Dudro at Ignatius Press suggested I write a book on Saints Louis and Zélie Martin, I jumped at the opportunity. Getting to know Saint Thérèse's family has been a wonderful journey. They too have become great friends and models. I hope the blessing I have received from writing this book will extend to those who read it.

Zélie was an avid letter writer and described events, facts, and her feelings in depth. I have drawn extensively from her correspondence, as well as from Louis' few precious letters and their daughters' writings. I have also used other sources including *A Family of Saints* by Father Stéphane-Joseph Piat, O.F.M. My most unusual reference was a book on Victorian lace that mentioned the 1858 Alençon exhibition and Zélie Guérin winning a silver medal. This shows what a talented lace maker Zélie was!

I am indebted to George Weigel for introducing me

to Ignatius Press and to his wife, Joan, for her assistance. Many people have helped me in writing this book. My sincere thanks go to Vivian Dudro, Gail Gavin, and Roxanne Lum at Ignatius Press, John O'Rourke at Loyola Graphics, and to many friends who have helped in various ways, including: Irene Elliott, Silvie Gallardo, Patrick and Elena Kilner, Madie Kilner, Ben Kilner, Erin Kwong, Michelle McGregor, Hannah O'Connell, Cecilia Ouyang, Tony Schiavo, William Simpson, Deacon Robert Vince, Elke Wojan, Thomas and Claire Wong, and Gianna Wong. I must also thank my other favorite saint, Saint Notburga; her inspiring story helped me get to the place in life where I could write this book.

My family has been a big part of this journey. I thank them for all their support. My father and my brother Edward helped me in ways too numerous to mention. My sister, Emily, and my brother Lawrence read the manuscript and provided helpful comments. I am very grateful to my mother, who edited and proofread multiple versions.

Finally, a huge thank you to my dear friend Eleanor Simpson. Her critiques and suggestions helped shape the story, and her encouragement and technical assistance helped make this book possible. Without her, *Louis and Zélie: The Holy Parents of Saint Thérèse* would never have been brought to fruition.

A. M. D. G.